Land

A Stranded Novel

By Theresa Shaver

Acknowledgements

When I was fourteen years old an eagle eyed librarian saw me sitting at a table bored out of my mind during a spare. She marched over and thrust a book at me and told me abruptly to read it, that it would change my life. I was bored enough that I did and all I can say is WOW. Who knew that there were all these amazing lives and stories happening in books. Ever since then I have been devouring books as fast as I can get my hands on them. So Thank you gruff librarian for getting me started. If I didn't have a book to read I would make up elaborate stories in my head (Me starring in them all!). So after waiting for my favorite authors to hurry up and write the next book, I started writing down the one in my head. My husband, who loves me uncontrollably but isn't much of a talker, read some of it and said, "I like it." He has been given the title of VP of Silent Encouragement. Thank you Derek. Thank you for believing in me. A good friend, Jennifer Cotie Ford cleaned the whole raw mess up and we shall call her Editor Extraordinaire. Thank you Jen, I will never forget sharing the creation of my first book with you. Ok Ok to the little people that keep poking at me and whining are you done yet? I'm done but I wouldn't have been able to do it without you guys reminding me every day how much fun make believe can be. I love you Monkey one and Monkey two now go and play. I have to start book two.

To the reader, OMG thank you for buying my book! I could fill the rest of the page with that sentence. I really, really, REALLY want to know what you think. Please take a couple of minutes and review this book on Amazon. It will help me write better and did I mention I really want to know what you think. So even if you hated it.....review it!

Chapter 1

Alex looked around at the bright, overly decorated buildings on Main St. Disneyland and gave a sigh as she pushed a golden red curl out of her green eyes.

"This would have been a lot more fun if we could have been here when we were ten." she said, turning to her best friend Emily.

Emily was busy scrolling through her IPhone and didn't even hear her. Alex was glad that they were going to have a chance to spend some time together. It seemed to her that they had hardly spoken in the last three months since Emily had started dating Mason. Growing up together on neighbouring farms in Alberta, they had been inseparable since they got on the same school bus for their first day of kindergarten. They had grown up with all the same interests and hobbies until age thirteen, when Alex started to get serious about gymnastics and Emily decided swimming was her favourite. Even different sporting schedules had not deterred them from BFF status. But now at sixteen, it seemed there was finally a huge obstacle in the way of their friendship.

Alex looked over at Mason and his group of friends standing apart from the rest of the class. As always, Mason was holding court and Lisa, the ``prom queen`` wannabe along with Mark, the ``bully sidekick`` were hanging on to the football quarterback`s every word. Alex could understand Emily`s attraction to the guy. He was tall and broad with sun streaked brown hair that fell over his forehead in a dreamy kind of way. His eyes matched his hair, a golden brown hazel surrounded by eye lashes any girl would kill for. So yeah, standing here looking at Mason, any girl would get a flutter as long as you just looked. Within minutes of talking to the guy though, that flutter should turn to stone. Mason was one of those jocks that was all about himself and needed constant adoration. Once again, it baffled Alex as to why her best friend was dating the jerk. Both girls were on the honour roll and volunteered for extra credit. Emily having way more patience, had started tutoring and that`s how the Mason thing started. After a week of tutoring Mason, Emily had started walking the halls, holding hands with him and sitting with his group at lunch. When Alex had tried talking to her about it she had brushed Alex off, saying that she was too judgmental and if she really knew Mason she would like him too.

After that Emily drifted further away and rarely did anything with Alex. "I really miss her but she has changed so much." thought Alex.

Looking around at the rest of her class she saw some of her other friends in a group and realized that the class was divided mainly into two groups, farm and town. With another sigh Alex thought about how Emily wasn`t really in the farm group anymore.

Mr. Carter was trying to get the class to move closer together so he could give out the schedule for the day and wasn`t having much luck. The kids were excited and distracted by being in Disneyland. It still amazed Alex that somehow her class won this trip by having the highest test scores in the whole province. Bringing more than twenty teenagers to California seemed a little crazy to Alex even with three teachers and two parent chaperones. When she first found out about the trip, Alex didn`t really want to go. She figured it would be a bit of a gong show with some of the town kids getting out of control and she felt Disneyland was made for a much younger crowd. Surprisingly it was Emily who convinced her to come, saying it would give them a chance to reconnect and spend time together.

Emily had said that she would really like to room together in the hotel. Alex was really happy to hear this because she had heard Lisa telling another girl that she and Em were going to room together and Alex had been jealous not to be rooming with her friend.

Last night in the hotel, Alex and Emily stayed up late and talked about a lot of things that had happened in the last few months. They felt reconnected after not spending time together. Alex talked about her gymnastics and other things in her life and Emily confessed her confusion over Mason.

"I don't think I'm ready for what he wants. He suggested that this trip would be a good time for us to "take the next step" but we've only been dating for a few months and I'm not sure I want to go there yet." Emily said with a frown.

Alex was used to her friend being more assertive and sure of herself so she tried to help.

"Just tell him how you feel and make it clear so there's no confusion." she advised.

Emily grimaced, "You don't know Mason. He doesn't like to be told no. I'm just so glad you decided to room with me. I overheard him telling Lisa that he'd let her know what night he wanted her out of the room. I didn't want to let that happen so thanks again for staying with me." she smiled gratefully at Alex.

Alex was shocked. That's why Emily wanted her here, to run interference? After the disappointment and loneliness of the past few months without her friend, Alex was mad and blasted her friend.

"Really Em?! That's why you convinced me to come, so I could protect you from your bully of a boyfriend? Really? How stupid am I that I thought you missed me and wanted to spend time with me? Unbelievable! Well if that's all you need me for, then forget it! You're my best friend but three months ago you dumped me for a guy. A guy who you can't even say no to, you can't treat me like that and then expect me to just snap to it when you need help!" she turned away with frustrated tears in her eyes.

Alex stared at the hotel's bland wallpaper waiting for a response from Emily. When none came she whirled around ready to yell and saw her friend staring down into her lap with tears flowing down her face. All the anger left Alex and she slumped down beside her and put her arm around her shoulder. They sat like that for a while until Emily composed herself and started to quietly talk.

"You're right Alex. I owe you an apology. I have put Mason ahead of you and I'm so sorry. He really isn't a bully. He's just strong willed. I really like him. He's so different when it's just the two of us together. I know if you got to know him you'd see a different side of him. Please Alex, forgive me? I didn't just ask you to room with me to put him off. I really miss you and wanted time with you too. Please understand."

Alex sighed in frustration, "I can't get to know him if we never hang out Em. I miss you, we all miss you. I promise to make the effort to get to know him better if we start spending time together again. I love you and just want my BFF back, Ok?"

Emily brushed her tears away and threw her arms around her best friend. They spent the rest of the night gossiping and giggling.

Alex smiled at the memory and looked around at her classmates. She found herself meeting the dark blue eyes that belonged to Cooper Morris. The amused mocking smirk on his face made Alex quickly look away. She didn't know why Cooper always made her feel nervous but found herself often looking in his direction at school and it seemed that most times he was looking right back. Cooper had the bad boy rep at school, dressing the part with a beat up leather jacket, his black hair, dark blue eyes and a devilish grin. It seemed to Alex that it was mainly rumours but it wasn't like they hung out with the same people so she didn't have a lot of firsthand knowledge about him. After Emily's comment about Alex being judgmental, she was going to try harder to have an open mind about people.

She kept looking around to see if they were going to be allowed to head deeper into Disney when she noticed Quinn and Josh heading in their direction. The boys were good childhood friends of Alex and Emily and had spent a lot of time while growing up together camping and hanging out at the lake, working on Four H projects. The third boy that usually completed their group was David but Alex didn't see him nearby. She wasn't really surprised, as

David had been in love with a clueless Emily for forever and he tended to avoid her since she started dating Mason. The boys had also felt Emily's absence in the past few months and were happy to see her and Alex had made up.

"Hey guys! Any idea where you want to go first?" asked Quinn

"I'm hitting Space Mountain until I feel like puking and then I plan on finding Goofy and hurling all over him!" Josh exclaimed.

Alex groaned but had to laugh as it was so typical of Josh and his rough and crazy personality to make such a statement. Quinn punched his friend in the arm and joked, "If you change that to Mickey Mouse, then I could get on board with that plan."

Josh was of medium height and stocky, with a barrel chest and thick muscular arms that he had developed from the hard work he put in on his family's farm. He had curly brown hair and brown eyes that always seemed happy. Quinn had the height and build of a football quarterback, tall and broad with his own muscles. His hair was wavy blond and he had calm blue eyes.

Alex was watching her teacher impatiently, "Looks like Mr. Carter isn't having much luck moving the class together and he's going to each group and giving the schedule out." Alex pointed out.

"Finally! I'm ready to rock this play land." Josh said.

For the first time, Emily looked up from her IPhone and joined the conversation, brushing her long blond hair back impatiently.

"Hey guys, I've been reading the headlines online and something weird seems to be going on." With a worried expression she explained, "The US government has gone to DEFCON 2 and the news is saying that that means nuclear war is the next step. CNN is saying the last time they went to that level was during the cold war."

"No way man! That would be just our luck. We're like 1500 miles from home and in one of the guaranteed cities that would take a hit!" Josh joked.

~ 5 ~

"I don't think this is a joke." Emily said seriously. "I think we should tell Mr. Carter about this. I'm really worried."

All the kids in Alex's group turned to look for their teacher and saw him coming towards them. A few steps away and the man seemed to stagger and freeze with wide eyes. Then he swayed and finally toppled to the ground.

To Alex it seemed as though all sound was sucked out of the world in an instant. Then kids were screaming and yelling and racing towards their teacher. Quinn got to him first and Josh was yelling at Emily to call 911. Alex felt like her feet were glued to the ground. She was looking around Main Street Disney to see if she could spot any security or employees when the realization came to her that this situation was way bigger than her fallen teacher. She could hear plenty of excited voices but nothing else. The music was gone. The sounds of rides, cars, phones ringing, all mechanical sounds where gone, even the huge water fountain in the middle of the square had stopped gushing, the water slowly draining away. At that moment, movement in the air caught her attention and she looked up unbelievingly. A huge airplane was slowly falling out of the sky. It looked like it would hit the ground a few miles away. Alex clutched Emily's arm and pointed up at the plane, still unable to speak. Emily looked up from her dark phone and her mouth dropped open with a whimper.

At this point, Quinn was doing CPR on Mr. Carter and looked over at Emily to see if she was calling 911. As he was about to yell at her, his gaze went up to see what the girls were looking at in terror. When the plane registered in his mind he fell back on his butt and cried out, "NO!"

It seemed that everyone around them was now watching the falling plane. It took what felt like forever for it to finally pass below the horizon but seconds later the explosion was easy to see and hear. Emily turned away and buried her tear streaked face against Alex's shoulder. Alex was numb with disbelief. "We're at Disneyland. This doesn't happen at Disneyland!" she thought. She gently pushed Emily back and took her phone out of her hand. It was off so she tried to turn it on but nothing was working. She looked around to see if anyone else had a phone and could see lots of other students staring at cell phones that didn't seem to be working.

Someone close by was screaming and it felt like a drill in Alex's ears so she tried to find the source and wasn't that surprised to see the youngest teacher, Ms. Scott belting it out while pulling her hair on both sides of her head. Just as Alex thought she should go get her calmed down, Mrs. Moore, who was the oldest of the teachers and quite the battle axe, grabbed the younger teacher by the shoulders and gave her a quick shake with a stern "Settle down!" When that didn't work she just gave the young teacher a slap across the face. Instant silence from the screaming was the result and Mrs. Moore shoved the shocked teacher at one of the parent chaperones and told her to get her settled down.

With her hands raised in the air she loudly ordered, "All Prairie Springs students form up on the grass and sit down...NOW!" the last word said with a louder snap. As Mrs. Moore saw students moving onto the grassy area by the street she turned and looked to Alex's group. Quinn was still sitting on the ground beside Mr. Carter and Emily had knelt down on the other side of him and was holding his limp hand. Alex and Josh were standing staring down at him not sure what to do.

Mrs. Moore moved over to them and took a deep breath. "Quinn?"

He looked up at her with a stunned expression on his face and tears shining in his eyes and said, "I think he's dead."

Mrs. Moore leaned over and placed a comforting hand on his shoulder and said in a calm voice "Yes. There was nothing you could have done for him Quinn. He had a pacemaker and it would have stopped as well. But thank you for trying. You are a good boy."

"I don't understand. What do you mean it would have stopped?" Quinn asked confusion on his face.

"Yes, well. Please join your classmates on the grass and I will try to explain what I think is happening." Mrs. Moore offered.

As Quinn got up off the ground and Alex helped Emily up, Josh was shrugging out of his sweat shirt and went to cover Mr. Carter with it. "Josh, don't do that!" Mrs. Moore barked. At Josh's expression Mrs. Moore softened and said in a kinder tone "That is very respectful of you but we must be practical. You will need your sweater later." With a confused face Josh stepped back and put his sweater back on. Mrs. Moore leaned down and pulled Mr. Carter's jacket up over his face. She then took his money belt off and retrieved his wallet from his pant pocket. She dropped both items into her purse and ushered the group over to the subdued students sitting on the grass. Once they were seated, she took in the whole group and lowered herself to one knee.

"A terrible event has happened and there is no way for me to know the exact details but from what we have seen I can guess what has happened. It appears all electronics are not working and as we saw with the plane falling and crashing many mechanics have also failed. That could only be caused by an EMP. That means an electro-magnetic pulse. This happens when a nuclear device is detonated."

The uproar that followed was full of confused shouts, yelled denials, loud sobbing and wailing. Mrs. Moore raised her hands and waited for the crowd to calm down and was about to speak when Emily stood and turned to the group and loudly stated "I was watching the news on my phone before it went out!" as everyone was now focused on Emily she lowered her voice and told what she had seen on CNN then quickly turned around and sat back down.

"Well that certainly makes things somewhat clearer. Thank you Emily, for that information. So we have some important decisions to make and we must make them fairly quickly." Mrs. Moore scanned the group to see if they were following her words and then continued.

~ 8 ~

"Everything will be different now. We cannot count on the government to take care of us. We will have to take care of ourselves and that means working together. We won't be able to fly home now so we have to decide if or how we will get back to Canada."

Suddenly Mrs. Davis, a parent chaperone, jumped to her feet and said "What are you talking about? Of course we will go home! The authorities will get this straightened out and get us home. We must be patient and wait for help. All this talk of not counting on the government is irresponsible of you. It will only panic the children. I suggest we return to the hotel and wait for the management to sort this out!" she finished while looking around the group for support. Everyone stared at her and then swung their eyes back to Mrs. Moore to see what she would say.

Calmly Mrs. Moore tried to explain the situation. "Mrs. Davis, I understand your reasoning but this is not a normal situation. We can walk back to the hotel but please understand. There will be no power to the elevators so that means climbing 10 flights of stairs as that is the floor we are on. Also, the room doors all have electronic locks that won't be working so we will have to break the doors open. It will also be very dark in the hallways with the lights out. Next, the management and staff are just people like us that will most likely all leave to check on their own families. With almost all transportation not working, the government will not be able to move around to help most people. Therefore as I said, we must take care of ourselves. This will be a huge challenge. Food and water and safety must be our first priority. With no electricity the water will not flow. With no transportation, food will not be delivered. And finally with over ten million people in this area and no real law enforcement, within days this city will explode with violence. We know of one plane crash but there were probably more which means fires. With the roads blocked by broken down cars and fire trucks not working anyways, the fires will burn out of control. Does everyone understand what I'm saying? The best thing we could do is try to leave this city as soon as possible." and with that final statement Mrs. Moore sat down.

Chapter 2

Alex looked at her watch and was surprised to see that only 20 minutes had passed since all this started. It was only 8:30 am and it felt like late afternoon to her.

"Does your watch work?" came from over her shoulder. She turned and saw it was Quinn asking.

"Yes it's only 8:30." she told him.

"Why do you think your watch works? Mine is dead. It was a digital I got last year." he asked.

"Don't know but maybe because it's really old. I have to wind it every morning. It was my Grandmother's."

"Good to know. Some really old stuff might still work." he replied with a smile.

"Listen, if this is what Mrs. Moore is talking about and after what Em saw on CNN it sounds like it is, we really need to come up with a plan and I don't think we should take too long." Quinn advised.

Staring into Quinn's eyes, Alex couldn't help but wonder how he seemed so calm. Living on a farm meant you learned to keep your head in the game and make quick decisions. Working with animals is always tricky and can be unpredictable. But this was so far from anything they could relate to that Alex felt like she was barely holding on. The one thing she did know was that she trusted Quinn a hundred percent. They had been friends forever and he'd always had a good head on his shoulders. Even when Josh was doing crazy stunts or pranks, Quinn could always steer the situation the right way so everything worked out. Alex always thought that sometime in the future she and Quinn would end up together as a couple. It just never seemed to be the right time and they were always so comfortable together that there was never any pressure to be more than the good friends they were.

A sudden thought jumped center stage into Alex's mind. "Oh my God! What about radiation. Don't we have to think about radiation if a nuclear bomb went off!" she gasped.

"Whoa, Ok, hold on. Other than that plane crashing no one saw an explosion or heard anything. No mushroom cloud on the horizon like you always see in the movies, so what ever happened, it wasn't that close but yeah definitely something to keep in mind." he consoled.

"Right now we are in the middle of millions of people and that is really far from my comfort zone. So the sooner we get out of here and into the country side, the better I'll feel. Let's grab the rest of the gang and talk to Mrs. Moore. No one else seems to be getting it together so let's talk to her and see if she has a plan."

Alex went over to get Emily who was talking to Mason and his friends. When she told Emily what she and Quinn had discussed, Mason jumped in and said they would come talk to Mrs. Moore as well. With a shrug Alex turned away and headed back to Quinn who had rounded up Josh and found David as well. As her group of students approached Mrs. Moore, Alex noticed others heading the same way. Cooper and Dara, a girl from town with black hair with bright blue streaks running through it joined up with Quinn's group. Alex arrived in time to hear Quinn ask Mrs. Moore how she knew so much about nuclear bombs.

"Well Dear, I'm a Prepper and have been for years. If you don't know what that is I will explain. There are a lot of people who believe that the world as we know it will someday change drastically. Whether it is a pandemic of some sort, an economical crash or nuclear war, civilization as we know it will end and chaos will ensue. So we prep for it. Knowledge is a Prepper's biggest asset so we research different scenarios and plan for as much as we can so that we will hopefully survive. I must say that for all the prepping I have done over the years, being at Disneyland was not one of the options I was prepared for." Mrs. Moore seemed to be reflecting on that statement and was clearly not pleased. She seemed to center herself and focused back on the group of students surrounding her.

"Alright students, time to make a plan. The best chance of survival is to get away from large populations and that means cities. So as I'm sure no cars are working that means walking. Now it might seem impossible to walk all the way back to Canada but it isn't and people have walked even further. That of course is the worst case scenario. Next would be bikes. Students such as you should easily be able to bike a hundred kilometres a day but probably quite a bit more than that. The best case would be if you could find an older vehicle. Anything in the 70's and older should work just fine. The problem with newer vehicles is that they rely on electronics so they would have shorted out. Older cars don't have many electronics in them so that is good. The bad news is we have to find them."

As she paused to catch her breath Mason jumped in with a question. "So you really don't think there would be any government coming to help?"

Surprisingly it was Dara who offered an opinion. "I like to read apocalyptic books and in every one it's always the people who got out of the cities fast or are already in rural areas that survive. The people who stay in cities, almost always die." she finished.

With a sneer on his face, Mason's friend Mark who was best known as a bully said, "Shut up Freak. No one cares about your dumb Goth punk books."

Dara shook her head with disgust and took a step back. Emily was looking at Mason to say something to his friend but he had a small smirk of his own. Lisa gave a quick giggle but sucked it back when Mrs. Moore glared at her. Quinn took a step toward Mark with an angry face just as Alex loudly called out, "You ass!"

Mrs. Moore took a quick step, blocking Quinn and declared, "Yes. Yes, he is an ass." This made everybody stop and stare at her in shock. No one could believe that a teacher had said such a thing.

"My goodness that felt wonderful! I've wanted to say that ever since I met you young man." she exclaimed to Mark. "Do you really think now, in this situation, that type of petty bullying is helpful? No don't answer. Just stand there with your trap shut and let me tell you something. What Dara said is the exact truth of the situation. You would not know that nor understand as you mainly read comic books. So....Hush!"

It was very difficult for Alex not to burst out with laughter at the expression on Mark's face. With his red hair and fair skin he looked like a tomato that was about to burst. Mason finally stepped in and gave his buddy a jab in the ribs with his elbow and a quick shake of his head. Mark took a step back and kept his eyes on the ground as he tried to cool down.

"Now as I was saying, we should leave here as soon as possible. I would not bother going back to the hotel as it is in the wrong direction and we have the important things such as money and passports with us. Clothing can be replaced. Time cannot. We should walk northeast until we find a sporting goods store and then buy backpacks, camping supplies and bikes if we can. Money should be working for a few more hours before people start to understand the situation. Some form of weapon should also be procured. Things will get very dangerous and it's best to be prepared to defend oneself." Mrs. Moore stated in a no nonsense way.

Alex couldn't help but be a bit shocked by Mrs. Moore. She had always been a very matronly lady and somewhat strict but this was a not at all what Alex would have expected to lie at the core of her personality. She had always enjoyed Mrs. Moore's classes as they tended to be a challenge with some good debates, but this was an altogether different lady.

"Mrs. Moore," Mason stepped forward. "Why would we try to cross two countries overland when we are so close to the ocean? We could find a boat and easily sail all the way back up to Canada. It would be much quicker and not so physically demanding."

Before Mrs. Moore could reply, Mrs. Davis and Mrs. Hardsky the parent chaperones, along with a man no one knew came up to the group. Mrs. Davis started up right away.

"Norma, this gentleman is also Canadian and he has advised us that our best option is to go to the Canadian Embassy here. They are required to care for us and see to it that we get home." she said triumphantly.

Mrs. Moore looked the man over and questioned him. "Where are you from sir?"

"Please call me Paul. I'm here with my wife and daughter from Toronto."

Mrs. Moore then started firing questions at the man. "The Embassy, is it not in downtown Los Angeles? Wouldn't you have to walk through a lot of very poor, possibly dangerous, neighbourhoods? Other than allowing us inside, what do you think the Embassy could do for us? Won't there be thousands of Canadians going there? With no transportation how will they send us home? And if they can't send us home, how will they feed us? Thank you Mr. Paul but I do not believe that you can answer any of those questions with the answers that would make it worth going there."

As she started to turn away from him, he grabbed her arm and with panic in his voice loudly stated, "It is their job! They have to take care of us!"

Mrs. Moore gave the man a very steely glare. "Unhand me and remove yourself from this area sir. Attend to your own family and I will attend to my students."

The man moved away angrily and Mrs. Davis immediately took up his case. "Norma really, that is the best idea. We can't be responsible for all these students in a crisis! We need to go to the authorities for help and the Canadian Embassy is our best bet."

Mrs. Moore sadly shook her head and looked around at all the students in the class. Everyone seemed to have been listening to all the discussions about what to do. Most students look unsure and confused and some were still crying. The only other teacher, Ms. Scott was still sobbing in the arms of another parent.

Mrs. Moore stepped away from Mrs. Davis and raised her arms. "Alright students, your attention please! We have been discussing the best way to go forward and there are two different opinions of the best course forward. We will discuss both with you and answer any questions to the best of our ability and then you will vote on what you feel is the best choice for each of you."

Mrs. Davis was incensed by this and turned to Mrs. Moore with, "You can't be serious! They are children and don't know what's best for them! Letting them vote is ridiculous and totally irresponsible!" she said in a huff.

"I disagree." Mrs. Moore cut her off. "They are all sixteen and older and after being informed, have the right to choose. After all, this decision may mean life or death for them and I am confident that they are mature enough to have a say in their future."

"Well MY daughter will not be voting anything! This is a decision for adults not children." she said forcefully.

"Very well Mrs. Davis as you are her parent that is between the two of you. But as the rest of the young adults are without parental representation they will make their own decisions."

She turned back to the students and noticed that a few were smiling and that Mrs. Davis's daughter was looking miserable.

"As I was saying, the first choice is that we will all try to walk to the Canadian Embassy in Los Angeles which is about 20 to 30 miles away. We will then hope that they will help us to get home." she paused looking at everyone's faces to be sure they all understood the scenario and then continued. "The other choice is to try to leave the city as quickly as possible and hope to find bikes or other transportation along the way. After leaving the city we would then continue our way north towards Canada.

Now, you have all heard the different discussions about both these options and I will try to answer any questions." she finished and waited expectantly.

Alex and the other students around her looked to each other and Quinn said, "Let's step away for a minute." They all moved away from their teacher and once again it was Quinn that started the discussion. "Does anyone here want to go to the Embassy?" he asked. Everyone shook their heads no and Mason and Mark made comments like "idiots" and "suicide".

"All right so we are all agreed that we need to get out of here and on the road." He quickly did a head count. "Ok there are ten of us to start and who knows how many others will want to join us. But if it's ten plus Mrs. Moore I think that would make a good team to work out duties like standing watch and camp chores. And we can rotate so no one has all the crap work." Quinn was about to continue when Mason jumped in. "Hey, who made you team captain? I'm the quarterback here and I don't agree with your plan at all and neither do my friends!"

Then everyone started talking at once and the group quickly split into two camps. Josh and Mark were starting a shoving contest when Emily yelled out, "STOP IT!"

It was such a surprise that everyone stopped talking and pushing and turned to stare at her. "Mason, Quinn we have to work together on this or no one will survive! Mason if you don't like Quinn's plan then tell us what you think we should do and we can discuss it. But no more fighting! The longer it takes for us to figure it out, the harder it will be once we get out there." then she sat down on the ground and waited. Mason looked like he wasn't too happy his girlfriend had called him out but took a deep breath and sat down beside her.

Once everyone was sitting again and looking to him he began. "OK I agree we need to get out of here but I think going thousands of miles across two countries is stupid. I say we head to the coast and get a boat. We sail it right up to Vancouver and then hike the rest of the way home." he said with a smug smile.

Quinn was looking at him waiting for more. When he realized that was it, he shook his head and said, "That's it? Go get a boat and sail it away? Haven't you been listening? Nothing works! Boats have motors same as cars. Even if you found an old one, what would you do? Steal it? We are going to try to buy bikes. Not steal them. Ok, so now you have stolen a boat. Do you have any idea on how to sail on the ocean? Man, come on! At least on land you can't drown and what about food and water? That's almost as bad as staying put and waiting for help!"

Mason gave him a look of contempt and told him, "I'm not a total idiot you know! I was thinking of getting a sail boat so it's just a matter of getting out of the marina and then using the sails. As for stealing it, well it's a brand new world and survival of the fittest is the new law of the land. We can stock up on food and water on the way to the coast and we can also fish if we have too. It beats killing ourselves walking or biking thousands of miles. My old man always says "Work smarter, not harder." Anyways that's what we are doing and I don't need to talk about it with you. If you make it home I'll be sure to have a cold beer waiting for you. You will really need it by then."

Before Quinn could say anything else Mrs. Moore called them back over to the main group.

Once they were sitting again she began, "Now that we have answered your questions it's time to vote. All those wanting to head to the Embassy raise your hands." Alex was shocked that all the students and adults except for Mrs. Moore and her and Mason's group raised their hands. With a frown of disappointment on her face, Mrs. Moore said, "And those wanting to leave the city?" The ten students with Alex and Mrs. Moore all raised their hands. That was it, eleven people to leave out of the whole class. With a resigned sigh Mrs. Moore continued, "Although I disagree with your decision, it is yours to make. Mrs. Davis will now take over and you may follow her directions. You ten students who are leaving follow me to the side." As Mrs. Moore started walking away from the main group, Mrs. Davis realized what that meant and immediately started objecting. "What are you doing? You can't leave! You children join the main group right this minute. You lost the vote so you will be coming to the Embassy!"

Mrs. Moore rounded on her forcefully and told her "Shut up! You are not their parent. They have made their decision and as the adult responsible for them I give it my blessing. I will know that at least some of my students will survive this. Now go back and prepare the rest to get moving." she finished while turning her back on Mrs. Davis in dismissal.

"Norma you can't talk to me that way! And what about the rest of the children? They are your responsibility as well." she said in desperation. The thought of being responsible for all the students erased the smugness of getting her own way.

With a look of exhaustion Mrs. Moore turned back and wearily said, "Mrs. Davis, I will be accompanying you and the rest of the students to the Embassy."

"But you don't want to go there. I don't understand you at all!" she said in exasperation.

"All the students are in my charge. And even though I strongly disagree with your choice, someone has to try and keep you alive and that seems to be me. Now please go back and get everyone ready to go while I talk to this group."

With a look of disbelief on her face, Mrs. Davis walked away.

"Well if we do make it home, I'm sure that one will have plenty to say to the school board! And I for one would welcome that if it is the worst outcome of this tragedy. Now we must make haste as time is slipping away! Have you all decided what to do?" Mrs. Moore looked to the group expectantly.

Alex couldn't believe what was happening. "Why aren't they listening Mrs. Moore? This is crazy. Please come with us!"

Mrs. Moore turned to Alex with a sad smile and said, "Alex I'm sorry, I can't go with you. Most people are sheep. They can't think for themselves. They will only follow and look to others to take care of them. You students are all leaders and I know that you will do fine without me. The rest will need to be taken care of and I believe it will be up to me to do that." She turned back to the group, "What have you decided?"

Mason began by explaining to Mrs. Moore his sailing ideas and Quinn explained his.

"Alright both are sound ideas. Are you sure that you won't stay together?"

At the boys and their friend's negative answers she said "I am positive that you would do better if you stayed together but there is also a better chance of at least one group making it. So that's that. Mason, there is not a lot of advice I can give you about sailing but I will say this. Work together as a team. Stay vigilant for danger and don't give trust easily to strangers. The best judge will be your intuition. Also be reminded that even though this is a new lawless land you are setting out in, you will have to live with the decisions that you make along the way. Help others when you can but always keep your group's safety as a priority. Good luck to you and may God watch over you." With that she gave him a pat on the back and nods to Lisa and Mark.

She turned to Quinn and said, "I don't know which group will have the hardest journey so all I have said applies to you as well. Your journey will be more physically demanding, so rest when you feel safe but don't waste time. The longer this goes on the worse conditions will get and the worse people will behave. Remember that it is a different world out there and some rules will have to change. If you feel threatened do not hesitate to take action and if you are truly in a situation where it is your life against someone else, act accordingly. Do not let that burden you deeply as you are not only saving your own life but probably others in the future. Do you understand what I am saying?" She looked around and met all of our eyes.

Alex spoke up clearly, "If someone is trying to kill or hurt us, we should defend ourselves and if it means that person dies we shouldn't fall apart over it. Is that what you mean?"

"Yes" was all Mrs. Moore said.

"Alright Mason, you, Lisa and Mark should go now. Stop at the closest convenience store and get a map and some water. The sooner the better, it's going to get crazy out in the city soon." Mrs. Moore stood to see them off.

"Emily is coming too." Mason announced.

Alex's immediate response was, "No she is not!" and turned to face Emily who was looking down quietly crying.

"Emily?" Alex asked. "What's he talking about? You can't go with them! You can't leave me." Alex cried.

Emily looked up and met her best friend's eyes, "I'm sorry Lex. I'm going with Mason."

Chapter 3

Alex stared off into the distance. She could see people walking along the monorail track away from the now stationary train suspended up in the air. "I would have hated to be stuck way up there when it stopped." she thought. She just couldn't understand Emily. After choosing Mason over her friends all these months and she was now choosing him for a life or death journey. Alex didn't feel like she knew her friend at all anymore. It felt like a piece of her had just been snatched away. It was bad enough that Mrs. Moore wasn't coming with them but now Emily also splitting away was just too much to bear. She had heard all of her friends trying to get Em to change her mind but it didn't sound like it was working.

A tap on her shoulder made her look around with hope that it was Emily but instead she found David with an unsure look on his face.

David was a great guy. A little quiet compared to Josh and not as outgoing as Quinn but a stable addition in their group. You could always count on David for anything. Most of the time you didn't even have to ask him, he just seemed to know what was needed. Alex knew that David had a thing for Emily. She didn't know if he was in love with her but definitely he had been crushing on her for years. When Emily had started dating Mason, David had been in such a funk that he barely talked to anyone. For the first three weeks he walked around in a sulk. It wasn't until Alex had talked to him about it and shared her feelings with him that he started to come around. They had both decided that Em was just trying out a new crowd and once she really got to know Mason and his jerk friends, that she would ditch them and come back to her real friends. That conclusion seemed to be very wrong now that Emily had made this huge choice.

"You okay?" asked David with concern.

Alex thought if she tried to speak she would end up crying so she just gave a tiny shake of her head. How could any of this be okay?

"Listen Alex I don't think she's going to change her mind. Even Mrs. Moore took a crack at her and had no luck. So the only thing I can think of is, I have to go with them. I don't think I could live with myself if I let her go off with those three assholes alone. What do you think?"

The only thing Alex could think at that moment was how could Emily be so blind to this guy? So instead of replying she just leaned in and grabbed David in a tight hug and breathed into his ear, "Thank you."

She felt David stiffen just as she heard a tentative, "Lex? Can I talk to you?"

Alex let David go and with a deep breath turned around to face her best friend. She couldn't think of anything to say to her so she just waited.

When it was clear to Emily that Alex wasn't going to say anything she began, "I'm so sorry Lex! I know you must think that I'm a fool or crazy but," at a loss for words she stopped.

Alex took pity on her friend and tried to help, "But why? I don't understand why you would go with them. You don't know anything about sailing and those guys are so self-centered. At least with us you know we would do anything to keep you safe."

"Well that's one of the reasons. I don't think they would make it on their own. They bluster and brag so much but I think they are pretty clueless outside of their shallow high school world. So I think they need help. And I know I don't know anything about sailing but I'm the best swimmer in the whole school. You know I was on track for the National's and then maybe the Olympics so that will help. I don't think Mark even knows how to swim. Alex I know you don't like Mason but I really believe he cares about me and will try to keep me safe. He comes off as such a jerk but when it's just the two of us he is a totally different person. Please I need you to trust me.

This is something that I have to do." she begged for understanding.

With a groan of frustration Alex replied, "I do trust you Em, it's them I don't trust. I know how stubborn you are under that mop of blond hair. How can I go on this epic adventure without my best friend and what am I supposed to do if we make it and you aren't there?"

Emily gave a cheeky smile and said, "You know what an adventure really is right?" and in unison Alex and Emily cheered, "Far away from home and fucked up!" both girls broke out in laughter.

Alex's older brother Peter had once told the two girls to be careful and safe when they went on their first solo camp out. And when Emily said it would be a great adventure he had replied with the famous line. The girls had never forgotten and anytime they started off to camp they would yell it out into the forest.

After they stopped laughing they just grabbed on to each other and held on tight. After a while Alex pulled back and stared into Emily's blue eyes. "Okay Em, I guess I get why you're going but it scares the hell out of me. The only thing that makes it semi ok is that you aren't going alone."

At Emily's questioning look Alex explained that David was going with them to sea. Seeing the embarrassed look on David's face she quickly put in "David is good with motors and thinks he can help get a boat started. And he's very worried about his mom and little sister. He thinks going by boat will get him home faster." She made that up on the spot. While not really a lie, David was good with cars, he was always working on his old Mustang and with his Mom being all alone at home with an eight year old to watch over he must be worried. It was all Alex could think of in the spur of the moment to help David save face.

Emily turned to David and gave him a quick hug. "That would be so great David. I feel a lot better with you along to help out." and she gave him a sweet smile. Just then the rest of the group joined them and Mrs. Moore took charge. After David told her he was going with Emily she seemed very much relieved.

"Time to go, we have wasted too much time. It has now been just over an hour and the masses out there will be starting to get nervous. Mason, Emily, David, Lisa and Mark it's time you got on your way. Remember everything I have told you and be safe. When you make it home please tell your parents that I am sorry I couldn't do more for you. Good-bye, or as you are going by sea, Bon Voyage." With that she turned away and discreetly brushed a tear away.

As Mason's group stood by waiting, Quinn and Josh said their goodbyes to David and gave some last minute advice. Alex and Emily just stood looking at each other. Finally Emily started with, "Well this should be a piece of cake."

Alex came back with, "Nah, a piece of pie."

And together, "Just not a banana split!" which was another childhood saying meant to break the tension. With sad smiles the girls gave another hug and whispered, "Love you. Love you more." To each other and parted ways.

As Emily walked away with Mason and his friends David came up and put his arm around Alex.

"Bring her home David and you. Both of you get home safe." David gave her arm another squeeze and followed Emily out of Disneyland.

Chapter 4

When Alex could no longer see Emily she finally turned back to her group to see what was going on. Quinn, Josh, Cooper and Dara were all kneeling around what looked like a map on the ground. Cooper and Dara, Alex hadn't even given them a thought but guessed now they were down to five they would be getting to know each other much better. Cooper was this bad boy by reputation but that was all Alex really knew about him. He must be somewhat smart if he had chosen to come with them. Alex decided to keep an open mind until she got to know him better.

Dara confused Alex. Up until grade six Dara was a part of her group. Her family lived on a nearby farm and she and Emily and Alex had been in all the same activities and clubs. The summer before grade six Dara's parents had gotten a divorce and her Mother and brother and Dara had moved into town. Things had stayed the same until half way through the school year when Dara had started distancing herself from the girls. She would sit alone at lunch and recess and barely speak to anyone. Emily and Alex had tried to keep her in the loop but Dara just kept pulling away. By the beginning of grade seven Dara was alone and Alex and Emily had given up. By grade nine, Dara was into black clothes and heavy makeup. She started coloring her hair weird shades and had gotten a reputation of being a Goth. Alex didn't think she was a Goth but wasn't really sure.

"Not that it matters anymore." she thought, "We are in this together." and Alex would take any help available.

Mrs. Moore was talking to Mrs. Davis and broke away to speak to Alex. Mrs. Davis was gesturing to the remaining students to get up and get ready.

She walked up to Alex and surprised her by taking her hand. With a very intense stare she exclaimed, "I believe in you. I know you and the others can do this. You will make it home." Shaken by Mrs. Moore's intensity but also strangely more confident Alex gave a firm nod.

"I want you to take this Alex." Mrs. Moore reached into her huge purse and pulled out Mr. Carter's wallet and money belt. She handed them to Alex and then took out her own wallet.

"Take out the money and give the rest back to me and take this as well." she ordered Alex and handed her the money from her wallet.

"Mrs. Moore I can't take this! What will you do?" Alex cried.

"Hush now and listen! Mrs. Davis has two thousand on her and all the other students and adults have money so that is all I need. Besides, this paper will be worthless by the end of the day. So take it and use it as soon as you can. Find a sporting goods store and get bikes and camping gear and water and food. Give all of it to get what you need and then get out of this death trap city fast. Now, one other thing before you go. When you get home and I know you will, if I'm not there that means I didn't make it," Alex tried to interrupt, "No hush and listen. This is important! Go to my home. Do you know where I live? It's not that far from your farm. Good. Go to my home and check the basement. It is full of supplies. If it has been cleaned out don't worry about that. Go back behind my old shed and there is a set of storm doors with a pad lock on them. The key is under the kitchen sink. The storm cellar was enlarged and it is just as full of supplies and there is also a living space in it. Now this is very important. Tell no one! No one! Not even your family. It is only to be used in dire straits. You must keep it safe for a time that is life and death. Do you understand? Being a little hungry from rationing is not an emergency. Starving to death is. There is food and medical supplies but if it is all used up, it cannot be replaced. Do you understand Alex? This is so important to your future."

Stunned, Alex agreed. "Do you really think it will come to that Mrs. Moore? Starving?"

"It is hard to say but people do terrible things when they are scared. There is plenty of livestock and crops where we live so it should be fine but there may be a lot of refugees from the cities. Then again, Canada might not even be touched by this but I doubt it. Anyway, time for your group to go." and Mrs. Moore surprised Alex again by pulling her into a tight hug.

Quinn and the rest were all standing and waiting for Alex, so she headed towards them and they all started for the front gates. Alex thought that it was ironic that here she was in Disneyland for the first time and she hadn't even gotten more than 300 feet inside and she was leaving again, never to return. Suddenly she whirled around and called out to Mrs. Moore, "Thank you! I always looked forward to your classes! Good luck!" Alex could see Mrs. Moore standing alone watching them leave, then she slowly turned away.

Alex caught up to Quinn and gave a brief smile and nod to Dara and Cooper as she passed them. He looked down at her and asked, "Ready?"

"Ready!" she replied.

Alex checked her watch and was again surprised to see that only an hour and a half had passed. It felt like forever since this all began. At only 9:40am it was promising to be a very long day. She told Quinn the time and he suggested they plan to have bikes by no later than noon. While the students had been organizing themselves, there had been a steady stream of people leaving the park but it had been fairly quiet. Some crying kids but no one seemed to be panicking. Alex guessed that it helped that it had happened so early and the park wasn't as filled up as it would have been later in the day. By the time the group got out past the parking lots and on to a main street, things were much different.

There were car crashes everywhere and plenty of people screaming and yelling. Many people had bloody clothes and obvious injuries. There were no signs of emergency services. With all roads blocked with traffic accidents and no cars working, no ambulances would be coming. Off in the distance there were quite a few smoke pillars rising into the air. "No fire trucks" Alex thought, "We sooo have to get out of this city." and she picked up the pace.

"Do you know where we're going? I saw that you had a map." she said to Quinn.

"Yeah, while everyone was talking Cooper popped into a souvenir shop and snagged one and he also grabbed a bunch of water bottles and snacks that the staff were giving away. He bought a cheap pack and stuffed it full. Smart guy, real quick on his feet that Cooper."

Alex looked back at Cooper and saw he was carrying a pack that looked like it would burst any minute. She flashed him another smile of thanks and glanced at Dara who just looked away. With a shrug she turned back to Quinn and asked, "Okay so where to?"

"Well just up here we are going to hit a road called Katella Avenue. Then we go East on that until we come to a freeway called Orange or 57. That freeway should take us as close to the outskirts as we can get then we change freeways again. We talked about it and decided to try and take the main roads today to get as close as we can to countryside but if they are too packed with wrecks we might have to detour to smaller roads. The problem is the more detours, the more time we waste. So we just have to wait and see how bad the freeway is." Alex nodded but was distracted by a group of bloody people up ahead.

"We should try and help them shouldn't we?" Alex asked, looking around the group for an answer. She was surprised by their grim expressions and silence. Finally it was Dara that answered Alex.

"Mrs. Moore talked to us about this while you were saying good bye to Emily. She told us that we would see many people hurt and that we would want to help. She said that there would be tens of thousands of people who are hurt along the roads and if we stopped to help everyone we would never get out of the city and we would exhaust ourselves and put ourselves in danger. She told us if we could clearly see a situation where we could help quickly and then move on that that would be the right thing to do but otherwise just keep going. I know it seems harsh but looking around I feel so helpless. I mean where would we start and when would it ever end?" she finished with a small sob.

Alex was about to drop back and offer comfort but she was surprised when Josh beat her to it. Not that Josh was insensitive, just that most times he was oblivious to others, especially girls. The pair dropped back a ways and talked quietly and Dara even gave a laugh at something Josh said to her. Alex turned back to the front and tried not to stare at the injured people they were passing. They had to go around a few cars that had jumped onto the sidewalk but it felt like they were making good time so far. They came to Katella and turned east. The road opened up and was wider than the one they just left. Alex could see many restaurants and big box stores. She kept her eyes open for a sporting goods store or anything that might sell bikes. There were just as many crashes on this street and they came up to a tangled mess of six cars all smashed together. There were three men working on pulling it apart. One of the men was half in a car and the other two were trying to push and pull a smashed BMW away from the smaller compact car that the man was halfway in. When the one man sawn Quinn and the others coming closer he jogged over out of breath.

"Hey, can you kids give us a hand? There's a little boy stuck in the smaller car and we are trying to get him out. He's OK but really scared. His Mom's in the front seat and didn't make it."

Without even answering him the whole group headed straight for the pile up. Finally they could do something to help and maybe feel less guilty for all the injured they had passed by.

"Can one of you girls get into the car with him? You are both much smaller than us and you could fit no problem. He's strapped into a car seat and we can't get the right angle to get him out." The man asked. "Hey Roger, back out of there, we got some help here."

The man that must be Roger wiggled back out of the small car and came over. "Thank God. I think the little guy is going into shock. We got to get him out!" The men looked at Alex and Dara expectantly.

"I'll go. No problem. Hey Josh give me your multi tool please." Alex volunteered.

"Yup, Alex is the right choice. She's really bendy." Dara said, surprising a laugh out of Alex. She didn't even know that Dara was aware of her gymnastic talents. With Josh's multi tool in hand, Alex crawled up onto the car and started looking at all the angles of entry. Finally she slid in all the way where the big man couldn't fit. Crouched in the passenger seat it was a tight fit with all the damage done from the accident. It almost seemed as though the car had been made skinnier as there was hardly any gap left between the front seats. There was still plenty of head room left but with the front seats squished together there was no clearance to squeeze through them. Alex examined the head rests and saw the little buttons on either side. Perfect, removable head rests. She quickly got them out and twisted back to drop them out the window to give herself more room. Alex had to work very hard not to look at the poor woman who was dead in the driver's seat. Thankfully she was slumped forward on the steering wheel and facing the other way. She turned to look at the little boy in the back seat and it broke her heart. His blond curls were limp and his baby blue eyes seemed glazed over. If not for the rapid rise and fall of his little chest, Alex would have thought he was dead. He had a few drops of blood on his forehead but it didn't look like he was bleeding, so it probable came from his mother. Alex looked around the back seat and saw a sippy cup, a soft green blanket and a baby bag on the floor. She reached back and snagged the blanket and cup and brought it into the front seat and tried to shake the glass off of it. After wiping the cup off with her shirt she turned back to the little boy.

"Hey buddy. My name is Alex and I'm going to get you out of your seat so we can get out of the car. Can you tell me your name?" Alex said in a soft sweet tone. No response came from the child.

"OK, do you want your juice? Are you thirsty buddy?" she kept trying. A slight flicker on his face made Alex think he was hearing her. So she handed the cup back and held it in front of his eyes. Slowly his little hands came up and took the cup to his mouth.

"Good boy! Have a drink and then we are getting out of the car. Okay pal?" she encouraged. After a long drink those baby blues met hers and whimpered, "Mommy?"

Alex tried to smile but all she wanted to do was cry. What would happen to this little guy? No mother, no way to find his dad, all alone in this harsh new world. Alex shook those thoughts away and told the child, "Mommy's not here right now but she loves you very much and asked me to help you out of the car. Okay?"

The little boy stared at Alex like he was deciding and then nodded his head. So Alex decided to get this done before he could ask anything else. Taking the cup away from him she grabbed the baby bag from the floor and stuffed the cup into it. She turned back to the front seat and stuffed the blanket in as well then shoved the whole thing out the window. Quinn was right outside the window and took it from her.

"Is he ok in there?"

"Yeah, I got him to drink and he's ready to come out. Can you stay here to grab him when I pass him forward? I'm going to have to jack knife into the back to get him out and then I'll pass him forward. It's really tight but I can get back there. Tell those guys not to do anymore car pushing. It might make things worse. Ok?"

"No problem. Are you sure your bendy enough?" he asked with a smile.

With a laugh Alex said, "Watch and learn pal!" and she turned and slid over the top into the back seat and popped back up in the back. Feeling very pleased with herself, it turned into a red blush of embarrassment when she heard a, "Nice view!" muttered from the front of the car. Quickly turning to the trapped boy she plastered a smile on her face and started working on his buckles. She kept up a steady stream of meaningless words about being at Disneyland and from Canada to keep the boy distracted. Finally she sat back frustrated. The buckles were jammed and she couldn't get them unhooked. Feeling something jamming into her hip she remembered Josh's multi tool and got to work with the knife.

"Sweetie, the buckle won't open so I have to cut your straps to get you out okay?" seeing the panic on his face she quickly reassured him with, "It's okay, I'm an expert at this stuff and we have a brand new seat for you. Okay?"

With another unsure look at her and a big fat tear rolling down his face the boy nodded.

"Poor kid." Alex thought, "I wish this hadn't happened to you."

After getting him to raise his arms up, Alex started to saw away at the straps. It didn't take long for her wrist to start getting sore and in her mind she was cursing Josh for not having sharpened his knife. After what seemed an eternity the belt finally parted and Alex could start on the next one. After the second belt came apart Alex had to stop and rest her wrist and she realized just how hot and thirsty she was.

"Hey Quinn, any chance of getting a bottle of water in here, I'm roasting." she called. Quinn had been watching her progress through the window and quickly ducked out and was back in seconds. He handed her the bottle and she drank it down greedily.

Quinn was half way through the car window trying to get a look at the baby seat. "Now that you have cut the straps on this side, could you just sort of slide him out?" he asked.

"I don't think so. I would need to cut one more strap and then I could get him out." she guessed.

"Well do your best. We really need to get out of here soon. These guys have been giving us some tips and routes to take and it's going to take us a few hours on bikes to get clear of the main suburbs." he prompted.

Alex turned back to sawing at the strap and before long she had the little guy free. His little pants were soaked right through with pee but it didn't bother Alex at all once he had his arms around her neck. It took some convincing to get him to go to Quinn but once he went it was quick work for her to be back on pavement.

Alex grabbed the baby bag and rifled through it looking for a new diaper and pants and was happy to find them. Dara came over and took both. She settled the baby on the sidewalk on top of the blanket and expertly changed him. The little boy seemed to be entranced by the blue streaks in Dara's hair, and he kept reaching up to softly pat at them.

Alex slumped against one of the wrecked cars and wondered what they would do with the little guy now. She could hear someone yelling down the road and once again was eager to leave this city. Quinn came up to her and said, "We have to get moving it's getting close to noon and we've got a long way to go."

Feeling so helpless Alex nodded and said, "What do we do with him?" just as Dara was bringing him over. The boy was reaching his little arms out to Alex with a smile when the yelling from down the road got closer. His small face seemed to freeze and he twisted in Dara's arms and started to bawl.

"Wow, now he starts to cry? After all that and now he's crying?" Quinn exclaimed.

Alex tried to take him from Dara but he wouldn't stop twisting to get down. She had just got him held tight against her when the yelling was right next to her. "JACK! JACK! I'm here buddy, Daddy's here!" A man pulled the child from Alex's arms and wrapped him tightly against his chest. The boy was clinging to the man and chanting Daddy, Daddy, Daddy repeatedly.

Alex was in shock. What are the odds of this child's dad finding him in this mess?

"Thank you so much!" the man said to Alex and the rest of the people standing around him.

"I've been walking for hours the route I knew my wife would take to get to Jack's daycare and I didn't think I would find them. My wife Allison, is she here?".

No one could meet his eyes and he knew that the worst had happened. He crumpled to the ground clutching Jack and sobbed out his grief.

The man who had asked for their help was talking to Quinn and they broke apart with a hand shake. Quinn waved his group back on the sidewalk. "Those guys are going to take care of them from here. We have to get moving so let's just go. Keep an eye out for stores with bikes and let's walk faster." and he started to walk away. Alex was the last to leave. She was staring at the reunited family and couldn't help but feel more hopeful. If one child could find his way home then she and her friends could too.

Chapter 5

The group made good time speed walking down the road and after fifteen minutes or so Cooper pointed out a big sporting goods store in a shopping area that was next to a home improvement store and some restaurants. They weaved in between crashed cars and groups of people standing around talking and crossed over the street to the shopping area. Once they were alone in the middle of the parking lot Alex called them to a stop.

"Okay guys. I'm guessing we don't want to steal anything if we don't have too, so let's check the money situation. Mrs. Moore gave me all of her money and Mr. Carter's too but I haven't counted it. Let's get a count and just pool it all to offer the staff in this store."

Everyone agreed to that so they pooled the money and Alex counted it out.

"Holy crap! We've got almost five thousand dollars here!" she exclaimed. Mrs. Moore and Mr. Carter must have had a lot of money on them because the students had only a couple hundred dollars each.

"Well this should make things easier. We just offer more than the price tag and no one will say no to that. Alex, put two thousand in a different pocket and don't mention it to anyone in the store." Quinn instructed. "Cooper do you want to try to do the deal, you got some smooth ways my friend?" he asked.

Cooper wasn't even listening. He was staring at a cop car over in the corner of the parking lot. Both of the front doors were open but no one was around.

"I think there are police over there on the ground." he said quietly.

They all had a good respect for the police in their town and Alex's brother was an RCMP officer and Dara's Dad was a City cop. After a quick look at her friends, Alex started to move towards the cruiser and they all followed her. The closer she got to the car it was easier to see that there was an officer on the ground. He had been shot and his chest was a mess of blood. She quickly checked him for a pulse and found none. The shock of seeing a dead body wasn't as intense for her after being in the car with Jack's mom. Alex guessed there would be plenty more bodies in the days ahead. Looking up at Dara she gave a shake of her head. The officer was young and had a surprised look on his face. Alex was going to move away when something made her freeze. His handgun was still in the holster on his belt. Dara must have been thinking the same thing because she squatted down beside the body and looked Alex in the eye.

"If people are already shooting cops, what chance do we have? We should take his gun and anything else we can use. We have to start thinking about protection right?" Dara asked.

Alex found herself nodding. Guns didn't bother her at all. Growing up on a farm you got used to seeing and respecting guns. Alex was a pretty good shot with a rifle and not bad with a shotgun, but had never fired a handgun before. She reached over and unsnapped the holster and removed the gun. There were other objects on the belt and she quickly made a pile of extra clips of bullets and a can of mace. The flashlight didn't work and Alex didn't think the baton was something they needed. Meanwhile Dara had pulled up the officers pant leg and was unstrapping another smaller holster and gun off his leg. She then got in the front seat and popped the trunk. As she got out of the car the boys came around from the other side of the car where they had been checking on the other policeman on the ground.

Quinn spoke up, "We should take…" and stopped when he saw the pile of goods beside Alex. "Good thinking. We stripped the other cop as well. This feels so wrong but I think we will need it more than they will now. Let's check the trunk and see if we can find a bag to carry this stuff until we get into the sports store." he said.

The trunk had a large first aid kit and more ammunition for the guns. There was a gym bag that they emptied out and filled with all the equipment they had collected. There were also some folded blankets so Alex took two and went and covered the fallen police officers. She tucked the blankets under the bodies to anchor them and briefly bowed her head and said a quiet, "I'm sorry." over both. She tried not to think of the men's families and said a quick prayer that they would be alright.

When she stood to go, the rest of the group was waiting and they made their way to the big doors at the entrance of the store. Just as they stepped up onto the sidewalk, a guy wearing a golf shirt with the stores logo came out and turned to lock the doors behind him.

Cooper approached him while the others hung back. "Hey man, are you the manager?" he asked.

Without even turning to look at Cooper the guy said, "Sorry the store's closed. Try back tomorrow." and turned to brush past him.

Cooper put his hand up in a hold up gesture and said, "There won't even be a store here tomorrow. Don't you know what's happening out here?"

The guy gave Cooper a weird look and said, "There's a power outage. I sent everyone home earlier and have been catching up on paperwork. I'm sure it will be back on by the end of the day." and he moved to get by Cooper again.

"Listen man, it's a countrywide maybe continent wide outage. We really need to talk." Cooper tried again. The man gave Cooper a look like he was a weirdo and went around him heading for the parking lot.

Cooper called after him, "Okay, but when your car won't start come on back and I'll tell you what's going on."

The man didn't even turn around, just headed for his car at a faster pace. The group waited on the sidewalk and watched the store manager get into his car. After a few minutes, he got out and stormed his way back to the kids.

"All right what did you do to my car?" he yelled.

"We didn't do anything. I tried to tell you but you didn't want to listen. Come over here and I'll tell you what we know and what we've seen." Cooper steered him over to lean against the wall of the store and proceeded to explain to the man what had happened earlier that morning and what they had seen on the trip so far.

The man didn't want to believe him but after looking over at the stand still traffic and many car crashes he started to waver. It was when he tried to use his dead cell phone and the kids showed them their dead phones that he finally seemed to believe. As he stood there stunned, Cooper told him what they wanted.

"Look the best thing for you to do is go stock up on all you can from the store and then get home to your family. That's what we are trying to do. This place is going to get hit by looters anytime now but that's not us. We have three thousand dollars to pay you. Let us in and we can stock up, get some bikes and get out of here. So what do you think? Make some money or watch it all get stolen by the next group that comes by?"

The man just stared at Cooper for what seemed like forever and then finally said, "Do you have cash?"

"Yes Sir!" Cooper smiled.

"Then let's get busy." He said as he turned and unlocked the door and held it open for the kids to go on in.

The store was dim but with many skylights in the roof there was ample light to get around and find what they were looking for. Cooper was telling the manager where they were going and what they needed for bikes and supplies as Alex approached them with the money. The manager counted it and stuffed it in his pocket and told the kids to take whatever they wanted and that he was going to pack his own supplies. They all headed to the bike section and picked out bikes and helmets. They found saddle bags and storage containers that fitted on the bikes in different ways. After that was done they all headed to the camping section and picked up back packs and other gear. They grabbed freeze dried camping food, two small camp stoves, fuel and three lanterns. Sleeping bags, ground mats, two tarps and inflatable pillows went into the cart. After the camping gear was done they all headed into the clothing and footware departments to find changes of clothes, jackets and new footware if needed.

Alex kept thinking that it would be a fun shopping spree if only the world as she knew it wasn't changed forever. After finding some body wipes and a change of clothes, she headed to the change rooms. She felt sticky and stinky. Her shirt was stained with Jack's pee and her pants had blood on the knees from kneeling by the bodies of the police officers. Alex quickly stripped down and washed as best as she could with the body wipes. Feeling much better she pulled the tags off of her new cargo pants and tee shirt. She had on her favourite low hiking boots and would keep them. A Tilley hat completed her outfit.

When she got back to the others they had all the bikes and gear close to the front door. It was obvious as they tried to divide the gear up that they couldn't take it all. They were trying to decide what not to take when the manager pushed his own bike towards the doors. Attached behind the bike was a double child carrier that was packed full of supplies and its clear plastic windshield on the front was zippered closed. Quinn and Josh looked at each other and headed back to the bike area to get one as well.

Cooper was looking thoughtful about something and said, "Be right back." and before the girls could say anything he headed out the front door.

"Where do you think he's going?" Dara asked Alex.

"I have no idea but if the other guys can rig up a carrier we could have room to take a couple of tents." as the girls got up to head back to the camping section the manager stopped Alex.

"Here take these." and handed her the store keys, "I'm not waiting around for you guys, so lock the doors when you leave and drop the keys in the mail slot. If looters come for the store the door locks won't stop them anyway Good luck getting back to Canada and thanks for paying me instead of just stealing things." and with that he was out the door.

Alex dropped the keys by the supplies and she and Dara grabbed another cart and went in search of tents. After finding what they were looking for and a few more things that they thought would come in handy they went back to the bikes. Quinn and Josh had gotten two child carriers and almost had them on the bikes. Cooper came in the front door carrying a few things and when he got to the group he dumped his stuff with the rest.

Seeing that he had been outside Quinn was surprised and asked, "Where did you go man?"

With a cocky grin Cooper announced, "Just doing a little looting for the common good. I went over to the home improvement store but there was no one there so I broke a window and grabbed some stuff we might need." Nodding down at the stuff he brought in, he explained, "We might need to get around roads if they aren't passable so I got us some wire and bolt cutters as well as two crowbars. I was thinking of chain link fencing and pad locks." he bowed for applause.

Alex couldn't help but smile at his cocky attitude and in truth it was good thinking on his part. The others thought so too and applauded him.

"Great job man, that will really save us time if we get stuck." Quinn praised. "Okay guys that's it. Let's load this stuff up and we can spread some of it around the backpacks. Everybody make sure the water bottle holders are full and take an extra bottle in your pack. Also we have four guns and a can of mace, so let's figure out who's going to carry them. Does everybody know how to work a gun?" he looked around to take a poll. All three of the boys had fired handguns before and Alex was surprised when Dara said she had as well.

"I guess that leaves me out of the club." she said. "I can shoot rifles and shotguns but I've never shot a handgun before so why don't I carry the mace and you guys take the guns. When we get out in the country we can have a practice."

"Sounds good," Quinn said "You shouldn't have any problem learning the difference and I know you're great at target practice with a rifle so we can sort that out when we hit the countryside."

They all got waist packs and stored the weapons and extra clips in them, except for Cooper who had taken the holster and belt off one of the cops outside. He pulled his shirt closed to cover it and then everybody got busy loading gear up. Within ten minutes Alex was locking the front door and dropping the keys in the slot.

"Well, shopping spree is over," she thought, "now it's time to physically pay for it." Hitching her backpack into a more comfortable position and tightening the straps, she climbed onto her bike and followed the others down the road.

Chapter 6

Four hours later Alex was definitely paying the price. Her thighs burned and her shoulders where the pack's straps rested were rubbed raw. She had gone through her bike water bottle for the second time and was in desperate need to relieve her bladder. She was very thankful that her bike wasn't pulling one of the child carriers and felt bad for the extra weight that Quinn and Josh were pulling.

They had come a long way with only a few issues. The Orange freeway was heavy with car crashes but luckily, except for a few spots, it was a wide 5 lane freeway that had open sides and in some places even a pathway that ran beside it. In one of the tight spots they had had their first problem.

A man wearing an expensive suit and standing beside a fancy sports car that was across two lanes tried to wave them down. When he realized that the group wasn't going to stop he jumped out to block the road forcing the group to come to a halt.

"Hey kid, I want to buy your bike!" he exclaimed.

"Sorry Mister, it's not for sale. Can you move out of the way please?" Cooper answered.

"Of course it is," said the man with a smirk, "everything has a price, name it and I'll pay it." he said waving a cheque book around.

"Really, we aren't selling, so please move!" Cooper said again with more force.

"Listen kid, do you know who I am? I've got an important meeting with the star of the next Lethal Action movie and I can't get my cell working. I need your bike to get to the studio, so how much? You guys have five bikes so you can double up."

When Cooper just stared at the guy shaking his head the man got angry. "How about I drag you off that bike and just take it you little shit!" the man spit.

Cooper leaned back on his bike seat and with a calm face swung open his jacket and rested his hand on the gun holstered at his waist.

"Mister I'm sorry to tell you this but your money doesn't mean anything and whoever you were yesterday you aren't anybody today. It's a new world and it's not pretty so go back to your worthless pop can car and let us pass before you get yourself shot. After we are gone, I would suggest you start walking but I wouldn't worry, I'm pretty sure your meeting is cancelled." Cooper told him.

The man blustered some more and cursed them all but moved back to his car. Cooper waved the rest of the group forward but stayed facing the man until they were all past and down the road. Only then did he give the angry man a nod and continue after his friends. They had made another hour of riding before their way was blocked again. An eighteen wheeler had jack knifed across the road and there was no way through.

After backtracking for ten minutes they found an open space to get off the freeway. Quinn made good use of the wire cutters that Cooper had stolen and cut away the chain link fence. They had to walk the bikes through and carefully down the embankment to the pathway, with one person holding back the fence so they could fit through. They stayed on the pathway paralleling the freeway for half an hour before it started to angle away so they found a way back onto the road and kept going. It surprised Alex how few people they saw. Most were walking and a few were sitting beside cars obviously hurt but most of the freeway was deserted. They did see two different groups that looked like family units on bikes. They were loaded down and had small trailers being pulled behind. Alex guessed that they had the same idea and were getting out of the city as well.

At one point they were in a tight area of the freeway and couldn't get off when they were forced to bike through a heavy cloud of smoke. On the other side they all had to stop and clear their smoke saturated lungs and stinging eyes. When their eyes cleared they looked over to the west of the freeway and saw a huge mega mall. It was on fire and burning out of control. It looked like a plane had crashed into it as the plane's tail was sticking out of the side of a Bloomingdales. All that jet fuel had ignited and the mall was a tower of flames and smoke.

No one else had tried to stop the group and even having to weave around wrecks they made good time. Every time they came to an area that was undeveloped Alex thought they had finally made it to the outskirts of the city, only to pedal into another suburb with row after row of housing and strip malls. Being from an area that was less populated it was hard for Alex to wrap her head around so many houses and people living so close together.

They were in an undeveloped area when Alex took a quick look at her watch and saw it was just after five o'clock. Even without her aching body and bladder Alex knew they needed to stop and discuss a plan for the coming night. She yelled ahead to the others and they all pulled up into an empty area on the side of the road.

"Sorry guys but I really have to go to the bathroom and anyway, we need to talk about the plan for tonight."

With groans of relief and aching muscles everybody got off their bikes for a pit stop. Grabbing a roll of toilet paper and some hand sanitizer from her pack, Alex headed over to some bushes to do her business. Everyone else took advantage of the break to do the same. When Alex got back to her bike she did some stretches and rubbed some ointment into her shoulders.

"That doesn't look good. I'll make some padding for your straps so it doesn't get any worse." Cooper commented as he came up to her.

Alex smiled her thanks at him and couldn't help thinking that he didn't seem like such a bad boy to her. The way he handled that jerk on the freeway had impressed her and he seemed pretty smart, always thinking ahead for what they would need. She rummaged through her pack, came up with a couple of power bars and handed one to him.

"How far do you think we've come?" she asked him.

Cooper thought about it for a minute and finally said, "I would guess about forty five or fifty miles so far. Not bad considering some of the detours. We were lucky that first freeway was a straight shot in the right direction. We should take a look at the map and see what's coming up so we can plan for when we stop for the night." He pulled the map out of his inside jacket pocket and moved over to the others.

While the boys were looking over the map, Alex went over to Dara who was searching through her pack and handed her the hand sanitizer.

"Thanks, that's what I was looking for." she said and coated her hands. "How are you feeling? My legs feel like wet noodles." she laughed.

"Tell me about it. I think we'll be paying for this tomorrow which really sucks as we will be biking even farther." Alex groaned. "I'm not looking forward to sleeping on the ground tonight. Do we have any Advil? Like by the case?" she joked.

Dara laughed, "Yeah, why didn't we hit a drug store before we started. There's that first aid kit we took out of the police car. Let's hope it has some."

The boys called them over to the map and explained the game plan. Quinn told them, "We did really well so far and we aren't that far from being away from the major suburbs. So I think we should try to go another twenty miles, so about two more hours and call it a night. We need to decide if we should camp out off the road or try for a hotel." He scanned the group for opinions and when no one answered he continued, "I think it would be safe for tonight to stay in a hotel. Most people would have been walking and will be tired so there shouldn't be any problems. It's tomorrow and the coming days that things are going to get crazy. What do you think?" he asked the group.

Alex and Dara looked at each other and said in unison, "Hotel!"

"Ok, keep your eyes open for something after about an hour. There's a junction coming up soon that we need to take north again and it's going to be going uphill more so we'll really feel the burn. We should try to be settled before it gets dark. With no street lights or business lights it will be hard to find anything after dark. So let's fill up the bike water bottles and grab a power bar and hit the road. The longer we aren't pedaling the stiffer our legs will get." Quinn said, standing and folding the map that he handed back to Cooper.

Alex was glad that no one seemed to have an issue with Quinn taking the lead and was again thinking that Cooper was a good guy. Dara still confused her. They had spoken more today than in the past few years and she wondered again what had caused her to leave the group all those years ago. Maybe on this long trip home she would get a chance to find out.

As Alex was adjusting her pack, Cooper came over with a couple of T-shirts. "This should help for now but I'll figure out something better when we stop for the night." he said while wrapping the shirts around the shoulder straps and padding them to protect Alex's sore shoulders. He tightened the straps, and in a surprising move, tucked a stray curl up under Alex's hat stepped back and said "All set. That should help for now."

Alex could feel the blush rising on her face and ducked down so her hat blocked his view. "Thanks." was all she could get out. She could see his feet turning away so she risked a quick look to see if anyone had noticed the unexpected move and came face to face with Dara's raised eyebrows. With her blush even redder she just shrugged her shoulders and started pedaling.

As the group got up to speed Alex let her mind wander. "What did that mean? Was he just being nice? Was he interested?" She felt like a silly girl that had just noticed boys for the first time. She had dated other guys and even made out a few times with them, so what was it about Cooper that made her so unsure and nervous. At that point Alex almost drove off the road so she shook her head and parked those thoughts for later, especially as she heard a small giggle coming from Dara behind her.

It was soon hard to think about anything except the road ahead and the burn in her thighs. She had lost all feeling in her butt a while back and counted that as a plus. They were definitely climbing higher and the pace they were going was slowing down. No one was talking, needing all their energy just to keep pedaling. It seemed like forever before Alex heard Josh wheeze out something. She hadn't lifted her head to look around in a long time, concentrating on the road ahead so she wouldn't run into any stalled cars. The road they were traveling on must not have been very busy this morning when everything stopped because the cars were spread out and most had just stopped. There weren't any crashes either, so it was easy to navigate. They hadn't seen any people around but after ten hours most would have walked away to find help. As she lifted her head and looked around she spotted what had gotten Josh's attention. Down the road about a half a mile was an old looking motel. It was one story and the doors all faced the parking lot in front. There was an even older looking gas station attached to it and what looked like a mobile trailer off to the side. The group pulled up just before the entrance and scanned the building looking for trouble. At least half the room doors were open to let the light in and there were some people sitting at picnic tables at one end of the parking lot.

"I'm about done with this bike courier job. So I think this is home sweet home for the night." Josh joked.

Quinn and Cooper exchanged looks and then shrugged. "I don't see any bad asses over there, just some tired people so let's check out the office and see what the deal is." Cooper said.

They biked over to the office and as they were getting off of their bikes an older woman came out to greet them.

"Hello there...Why, you're just kids!" the woman was surprised. "What are you kids doing all the way out here? she asked.

Quinn stepped forward and replied, ``Hello Ma'am, we are trying to get home but we`ve been travelling all day and can`t go any further. Do you have any rooms left that we could rent?"

The woman had a sympathetic look on her face and was nodding her head. "Yes, I do have a room left. It's a double so it would be a tight fit for the five of you but that's all there is. There have been so many people walking in from the highway. I haven't been this full in years. There's no electricity and the water isn't flowing but there's an old hand pump on the well back behind that you can use."

"That's wonderful." Quinn said. "Is it ok if we take the bikes in to the room? I'm afraid if we left them out they would be stolen by morning. We would pay extra for that." he asked with a boy next door grin.

The woman waved her hand dismissing that, "Don't you worry about that. Take them in and keep them safe. It's more important that you kids get home quickly than a little wear on old carpet. And don't worry about paying me. If it was my own kids out on the road all alone I'd like to think that someone would do the same. Besides I've made more money today than I have in the last two months." she said with a laugh. "Now what about food, it looks like you have some supplies in your little trailers, are you ok? I sold all the snack food and sodas to the other guests so I don't have anything to offer you."

"We're just fine for food and thank you so much for the room. I can't tell you how relieved we are, knowing that we will have a safe place to sleep tonight but please let us pay you. We have cash and it would only be fair."

Alex thought Quinn was laying it on a little too thick with the charm so she quickly stepped forward and handed the lady some cash.

"Which room is still open?" she asked, flashing her dimples.

"Oh, just let me get you a key and a bucket. You can send one of these strapping boys to fill it so you can clean up. The toilets will flush if you fill the tank. Hold on, be right back." and she turned back into the office. Alex gave Quinn an elbow in the ribs and rolled her eyes at his "Who me?" look.

The lady came back out and handed a key to Alex and a bucket to Quinn.

"There you go dear. It's the last room at the end. You come see me if you need anything else. Have a good rest." she smiled as they pushed their bikes toward their room.

The people sitting at the picnic tables were staring at them as they made their way towards the end unit of the hotel. An older couple and a mother and her little girl sat at one table with chip and snack bags and soda cans spread in front of them. The older man gave the kids a nod as they came closer. The other table had three men, one in a suit and two in dusty dirty jeans and tank tops. They were drinking beer and empty beer cans formed a pile on the ground beside them. The man in the suit was taking in the bikes and trailers with a thoughtful expression. The two greasy guys were giving Alex and Dara the once over. Alex felt a shiver go down her back at the leering looks and pushed her bike closer to the boys.

They got to the room and opened the door to a blast of hot, stale, cigarette tainted air. With no air conditioning and being shut up all day the hot California sun had heated the room up. Dara and Alex went in first and pulled all the curtains back and opened the front window and the small window in the back bathroom hoping for a breeze. The only thing that really did was give them some natural light to see the inside of the room. The girls moved the small table and chairs out of the way so there would be room for the bikes and then helped the boys bring them in and squeeze them into the front area of the room. This worked easier once Josh and Quinn unhooked the trailers from their bikes. It was so hot in the room that they were all sweating in minutes. Cooper grabbed a pillow and started fanning it back and forth in front of the door trying to get some hot air out of the room. He kept it up for a few minutes and then gave it up as a lost cause throwing the pillow back onto the bed.

Quinn went to the door and looked out as everyone slumped down on the beds with aching muscles. "I don't like the looks of those beer drinkers out there. If we are going to have problems, it will be from them. I think we'll have to post watches tonight just in case. Can someone make sure the bath tub is clean? I think we should fill it up now with the bucket so we won't have to go out back later. Once it gets dark, I don't think we should leave the room. Our bikes are worth gold right now and our supplies even more."

"The way those guys were looking at Alex and I, it wasn't the bikes they will be after." Dara said with a grimace.

"Good point. You and Alex should stay inside so they aren't tempted to start anything." Quinn said with a frown.

"Sounds good to me, you big strapping boys can fetch our water and Dara and I'll stay here and paint our toes!" Alex teased.

As if planned, the three boys lifted their arms and flexed their biceps in muscle men poses. After the laughter had died down Josh said, "How about you little women make us men some dinner?"

"Oh yeah, that would be great. I'm starving." Cooper chimed in.

Quinn was nodding his head too but then stopped to think, "We can't have anything hot. The smell would let everyone in this place know what we have. They probably only have snack food and the smell of hot food would draw them right to our door. So it will have to be a cold dinner." Groans all around answered that. After the work they did getting this far, they all wanted a good hot meal but they wanted a fight even less.

Quinn and Cooper went out with the bucket, leaving Josh to guard the door. Alex used some of her water bottle and a hand towel to wipe the bath tub out and made sure the plug was pushed in. The toilet still had water in the tank so it was good for at least one flush. They would have to remember not to flush it after every pee or they would go through the water very quickly.

~ 51 ~

Of the five one gallon jugs that they had brought from the camping section, half was already gone. They would fill them up in the morning and try to keep them filled every chance they found water. Five people on bikes went through a lot of water and Alex was worried about the next couple of days. The route they had planned would take them past Las Vegas and it was in the middle of desert country so water would be very important and she was worried that they wouldn't have enough.

Leaving the bathroom, Alex saw Dara pulling beef jerky and trail mix from the trailer, covering the freeze dried camping food with a sleeping bag so it couldn't be seen. Alex got out one of the camping stoves and fuel and a pot so she could boil water. Even though they weren't going to eat a hot meal they could have hot water to clean themselves up with and a hot drink.

Quinn and Cooper came in with a full bucket of water and went to pour it in the tub. Coming back into the room Quinn said, "This is going to take a lot of trips. That barely covered the bottom of the tub."

Alex followed them to the door and saw Quinn approach the table with the older couple and mother and child. After some conversation the man got up and headed to a different room. He came out with a bucket and went into the room beside his and emerged with another bucket. He handed his extra bucket to Cooper and the three disappeared around the back of the hotel. Loud laughter drew Alex's attention to the other table and she saw the three men still drinking. It seemed the pile of empties had grown and Alex wondered if the men had carried the beer from where ever they had been stranded. She saw that they were looking her way so she quickly backed into the room. She found herself hoping that they would drink so much that they would pass out and not cause any trouble.

It didn't take very long for Quinn and the others to come back with three full buckets of water and the tub was filling up faster. After one more trip the tub was half full and they decided it was enough for the night.

"We're going to help Mr. Thomas fill his tub up now. They're going to share their room with the mother and little girl out there. So give us about twenty minutes and we'll be in for the night." Quinn told Alex, Dara and Josh.

While they were waiting Alex and Dara used the steaming water from the camp stove and some hotel soap and wash cloths to clean off the dust and sweat as best they could. It wasn't a hot shower but after putting on clean shirts, they felt much better. Alex swapped out Josh from the door and he handed her his gun. She made sure the safety was on and tucked it into a pocket of her cargos. She stayed back from the door but had a good view of the drinking table. The older woman and mother and child had gone back into their room so the men were the only people outside that Alex could see.

On one of their earlier pit stops, Josh had gone over the basics of handguns with her and she felt more confident carrying it. It wasn't that different from a rifle and Alex was a great shot, having hunted with her Dad and done target shooting with her brother.

Josh had used the last of the hot water to clean up so Dara refilled the pot and set it on the stove for the other two boys to have hot water. The room only had two coffee cups beside the now useless mini coffee maker but they could take turns having a hot drink after they ate their meagre supper. While waiting for the boys to return, Dara and Alex set up the small table between the two beds for more seating and placed the food and drinks as well as the map on it. It was getting dark outside when Quinn and Cooper finally came in and emptied one last bucket full of water into the tub. Alex was surprised to see the time was almost eight o'clock at night. As the two boys got cleaned up with the hot water she got out the lantern and a fat camping candle from the trailer and lit it. Alex went to the door and took a quick look out, noting that the beer drinkers were gone. She shut and locked the door and then pulled the heavy curtains closed. It wasn't nearly as hot in the room as when they first opened it up but it was still very warm. Having the door open had helped to keep it cooler but Alex felt safer with it closed and locked now that it was getting dark. By the time she got the lantern lit everyone had gathered at the table to eat.

"Mm hmm, just what I wanted after a hard day's work! Beef jerky and trail mix. This sure will hit the spot." Josh joked sarcastically.

No one was happy with the supper but they all understood it was better to be cautious about advertising what supplies they had. As they were eating, they discussed what their plan was for the next day. Looking at the map and trying to figure out distances wasn't all that easy. Alex couldn't help wishing for Google earth to zoom in and see what was ahead of them.

She wondered if she would ever see a working computer with internet again, or if someday her future children would. It was those thoughts that finally brought the whole situation home for Alex. She had to quickly leave the table and race for the bathroom, barely making it to the toilet before throwing up what little she had eaten. Alex flushed the toilet and splashed some water on her face. She stood shaking in front of the mirror trying to get herself under control.

A knock on the door and Dara came in, "Are you alright Alex?"

Staring at Dara through the mirror Alex let out all she was thinking. "No more Google, no cars, no planes, no grocery stores, malls, cell phones, Facebook, new jeans, prom, Glee, no more iTunes and damn it, we will never see the last Twilight movie." she ended with a half laugh half sob. Dara's eyes had gotten wider as Alex listed the things that were gone.

"Oh My God! I think I'm going to puke." She covered her mouth.

"Feel free, I already did." Alex told her. "It just hit me. We've been go go going since the moment this happened that I finally realized that it's done. All the things in our lives that we took for granted everyday are over. If we want music we'll have to make it. If we want food we'll have to grow it. It's like we just got cast in a really bad Pioneer Village reality show."

"Oh shit, do you think we'll end up sister wives, pumping out babies and farming?" Dara exclaimed.

Alex couldn't help it. It was all too much to process and she burst out laughing and couldn't stop, even with tears rolling down her face. Dara started giggling and they both ended up howling with laughter and holding onto each other. The boys must have thought that they had lost it because none of them came to check on them. After they settled down and caught their breath they washed their faces and went back out to the main room.

All the guys were staring at them, afraid to say anything, and that set the girls off laughing again. The table had been put back and the food cleared away. There were two mugs of steaming hot chocolate sitting on the night stand between the beds and the girls immediately claimed them, sitting back on one bed to drink.

"Sooo, you guys ok?" Quinn asked. When Alex and Dara only nodded he continued. "Alright, Cooper is taking first watch until midnight, then me until three AM and then Josh until six. You two can have tonight off and take a turn tomorrow night. Josh will wake us in the morning and we should try to be out of here by six thirty. Hopefully the drunks won't cause any trouble and will be sleeping it off when we get away from here. I say we bike for an hour and then stop and cook a good breakfast. We are aiming for somewhere between the two small towns, Yermo and Baker for the end of the day. That's only the best guess we can make. It will depend on how the road is and what we run into on the way. It's going uphill a lot so that will slow us down. We also have to be careful about our water and keep an eye out to fill it up whenever we can. We're really lucky it's only April so it's hot during the day but not scorching. That's about it. We should get to sleep as soon as we can, tomorrow is going to be even harder than today was." he finished.

Alex and Dara made up two more mugs of hot chocolate for Josh and Quinn and Alex put a little more water on the camp stove for Cooper to have his on watch. When Quinn and Josh finished their drinks they laid down on the double bed closest to the door. Alex and Dara climbed on the other bed and settled down to sleep.

Alex was so tired that she thought she would be asleep in a second. The belly full of warm chocolate and soft bed should have done the trick but she couldn't stop thinking. Her thoughts were full of her parents and brother. "What was happening at home? Were they all ok or hurt? What if they were driving at the time and had a crash?" After a hundred what ifs Alex couldn't bear it anymore and switched her thoughts to Emily. "Where was her best friend right now? Did they make it to a boat? Would she be ok with the jerks she was traveling with?" Alex couldn't stop thinking and didn't think she would be able to sleep. After tossing and turning she gave up and just stared up at the ceiling.

She could hear Josh snoring and Quinn's breathing and Cooper shifting on his chair by the window. Just as she thought she might as well get up and do something like fill the water bottles in the bathroom, she felt her hand being held. Dara gave Alex's hand a squeeze of comfort and then just held it in the dark. Alex realized that her parents and best friend might be far away but she had a friend right beside her, one that she didn't even know she had been missing so much. With that thought, Alex fell asleep still holding her friend's hand.

Chapter 7

Everything must have been quiet during the night because when Alex woke up, there was a soft light coming in around the curtains and everyone was still asleep except for Josh by the window. Tilting her watch she saw that it was ten minutes to six and decided to get up. She tried to quietly slide off the bed but as soon as she stood up a groan came out at the pain in her legs and butt. Alex staggered to the bathroom trying not to whimper and it was made harder by Josh's muffled laughter. He obviously knew just how sore she was because sitting on the bathroom counter was a container of Advil and a bottle of water. Alex imagined that they all would be starting their day with the painkiller. While waiting for the drugs to kick in Alex put the lid down and sat on the toilet seat beside the tub. She started filling up the gallon jugs from the tub and topping up the bike water bottles. Once that was done she limped back out to the main room and grabbed some dried fruit and half a power bar to eat. Having thrown up her supper last night she was starving. The food took the edge off but she was definitely looking forward to a big camping breakfast down the road. They had enough food for all of them to eat for five days and after that they would have to start looking elsewhere. It would be a good idea to stop in a small town today and see if they could still buy some food. Alex still had almost two thousand dollars in her pocket and they might get lucky in a small town.

The others were all up by then and Quinn was passing out foldable camping toothbrushes that the girls had grabbed at the last minute from the store. It didn't take long to pack the trailers back up and Dara came out of the bathroom with an extra toilet paper roll and stuffed it into her pack. Then they quietly wheeled the bikes out to the parking lot and hooked up the trailers. Alex went back in and did a quick last check of the room to make sure they didn't forget anything. The pillows on the beds were tempting but with no extra room she wistfully left them and closed the door. Just as Alex turned from the door to get on her bike the older man that had lent them his bucket came out of his room. He lit a cigarette and walked over to the group.

In a lowered voice he asked, "Getting an early start, aren't you?"

Quinn seemed to think about it and replied, "Sir if I could give you some advice, things are going to get really bad. We came from Disneyland yesterday and nothing's moving. Planes fell out of the sky and burned with no one trying to put out the fires. We saw two policemen who had been shot. It's going to be even worse today. People are going to get scared and scared people do stupid things. No one is coming to help. I don't think anyone can come to help. You need to get out of here. There's no food here and when those drunken guys realize that there are no cops around, it could get ugly. You should check with the lady that runs this place and see if she has anything with wheels like a stroller, wagon or even a grocery cart and fill it with as much water as you can and then the four of you should head to the closest town."

The man puffed on his smoke and then dropped it and ground it out with his shoe before replying, "I think you nailed it son. I didn't sleep much last night thinking about it. I appreciate you warning me and I'm going to wake up the girls and get moving. Good luck to you kids. I hope you make it to wherever you are headed." and with that he nodded at the group and went back into his room.

As they biked out onto the road Josh started singing, "On the road again. Just can't wait to get on the road again." which was met by a chorus of "Shut ups."

For the first ten minutes it was very slow going. Everyone was feeling the effects in their legs from the day before but once their muscles warmed up it got easier. As they biked down the road Alex asked the group about stopping to buy food.

"If we stop at the first small town or service station we come to we might still be able to buy more food. Yesterday most people would have been waiting for help to come and still be fairly calm. As time goes by today, people are going to start to panic and make a run to stock up on supplies. If we stop early enough we might get in before the panic."

"I think you're right Alex." Cooper said and the others agreed. "Let's watch for a small town with a grocery. Service stations will have been overrun yesterday and most only have small amounts of grocery items. They mainly stock junk food. A small town food store will be better."

As their muscles warmed up they started making better time. There were lots of dead cars on the road but some had been able to pull off before crashing, leaving space for the bikers to get through. They passed by a few service stations with fast food restaurants and gas stations, but they kept going. Not many people were out and about but it was still fairly early in the morning. About eight o'clock they started seeing road signs for a town ahead, advertising privately owned diners and small businesses with nothing showing for the bigger chain stores. They biked past the exits and stopped about a mile past on a service road.

Quinn opened the conversation with his ideas, "I don't think we should all go into the town. Two of us should stay here with the bike trailers and three should go in. One person needs to stay outside the store to guard the bikes and two to go in and get what they can. Dara I think you should stay here with me. It's hard to say how nervous the people in town are and with your hair they might judge you as a wild child."

Dara was pissed off at that but understood that there are a lot of small minded people in the world and her punkish hair colour might make them wary. "Fine, but if it's going to be a problem then Alex, get me a hair dye kit and we can do camping beauty salon when we stop tonight." she said in a huff.

"Hey, I like your hair the way it is!" Josh defended with a smile.

"Thanks Josh, but Quinn's right. Getting home is going to be hard enough without us having to worry about small town red necks getting bent out of shape over blue streaked hair." Dara conceded.

"Sorry Dara and thanks for understanding. We'll stay here and try to repack the trailers to make room for anything you guys get. Empty out your back packs and saddle bags so you can fill them up in the store. Try for dried food and easy make stuff and get some drug store things if they have any. Try to go fast and be very polite, it might make a difference. Josh, keep the jokes to a minimum. These people may be trigger happy and we need to be in and out as fast as we can. So make like a good little farm boy and say "Yes Ma'am" and "No Sir" to everyone you see." Quinn warned.

"Hey, I can be respectable when I want to be!" Josh protested.

Everyone laughed and started to empty out their packs. Alex was half nervous, half excited to be going into a town. Other than the sports store they had shopped at yesterday, they had been avoiding contact with other people as much as possible. She hoped that they could get what they needed without any trouble. They helped Quinn and Dara move their bikes and trailers further off the road so they wouldn't be seen and then headed back towards the town.

Cooper and Josh both had guns tucked away where they couldn't be seen and Alex had her can of mace. Entering the town they were surprised to hear the sound of a truck engine. They followed the sound until they came to the main business section of the town where an old pickup truck was dropping men off up and down the street. The men all had hunting rifles or shot guns and were setting up to guard each of the business on the street. The men all watched as the kids biked past but they didn't confront them.

They biked into the parking lot of a fair sized grocery store that also had a pharmacy inside. There was a small line up at the main doors and six armed men blocking the way. Two of the guards were wearing sheriff uniforms and were talking to each person in line before passing them through. The kids parked their bikes off to the side in a bike rack and Josh stayed with them as Alex and Cooper got into line.

There was a commotion at the front of the line and Alex heard a man shouting at the guard. "I'm good for it and you know it!" She couldn't hear what the guard said to the man but he stormed away from the store.

Alex and Cooper exchanged worried looks. Alex was afraid that the guards were only letting locals in and that they would be turned away. When they finally got to the front of the line the guard looked them up and down and said, "I don't believe I've seen you kids before."

"No sir, we biked in. We would like to buy some food for our family please." Cooper told the guard with a respectful tone. Alex gave the guard a small hopeful smile.

It seemed like forever that the guard considered them when he finally nodded. "Cash only."

Alex was quick to agree, "Yes Sir, we have money."

"Let's see it. Everybody has to show that they have cash or they don't get in."

Alex pulled out the five hundred dollars she had in her pocket and Cooper did the same. They had split the money between them before coming into town.

"Whoa, that's a lot of cash for two teenagers to be carrying around. You two haven't been looting have you?" the guard asked with suspicion.

The look of shock on Alex's face must have convinced him it wasn't true because when Cooper told him their parents had given the money to them he waved them into the store.

They wasted no time and rushed through the main doors. Each grabbed a cart and headed to opposite sides of the store. Alex hit the breakfast food aisle first and zoomed in on the pancake mix. A five pound, just add water, bag of mix went into the cart as well as instant oatmeal. She had taken the pancake mix camping before and knew it was easy to make different versions by adding ham and cheese or dried fruit to it. A big bag of powdered milk mix went in as well. In the next aisle she grabbed as many instant soup mixes as she could, cans of tuna and ham. She continued grabbing dry goods like ramen noodles and bags of rice. Dried fruit like raisons and cranberries and apricots and a tub of peanut butter completed her cart. Alex headed over to the pharmacy area and grabbed pain killers and cold remedies as well as antibiotic lotion and sun screen. The hair and cosmetic isle was next and she picked out a dark chestnut brown hair dye kit for Dara. It was as close to her natural color as Alex could remember. A couple hair brushes, some shampoo, soap and deodorant went in as well. She paused at that point and tried to think of anything else they might need and how much room they would have to carry it. With a groan Alex remembered something her and Dara would definitely need in the coming days. She stopped her cart in front of the feminine hygiene section and grabbed two big boxes of tampons. They could take them out of the box and pack them around other items to make them fit. Another section caught her eye and made her think about the future. Without giving it much more thought Alex grabbed three boxes of condoms and stuffed them under some of the other groceries. As she was leaving the pharmacy section she had to pass through the baby supplies and she grabbed two bags of baby wipes. Heading to the front of the store she was going down the paper goods isle and she stopped to consider things again. A box of aluminum foil, a box of large and small Ziploc freezer bags and disposable containers, and a mini bottle of dish soap and scrub pad topped her cart. A hanging display of small bags filled with plastic zip ties would come in handy and she grabbed a couple bags of them as well.

When she got to the cash registers, Cooper had already paid for his load and was over at the customer service counter. Alex quickly loaded her goods on to the non-functioning conveyor belt and noticed canvas shopping bags hanging on the end in a display. She snagged a bunch and went to the man who was writing down prices on a paper pad to add up. When Alex realized how long that would take she interrupted him.

"Can I just make you an offer? This is probably around two hundred dollars' worth of stuff. How about I just give you three hundred to be on the safe side?" she offered.

The man looked at Alex with surprise and said, "Are you sure? That's a lot of money to just be giving away."

With a sweet smile Alex told him, "I know but I really want to get back to my Mom. She's not feeling well and I don't want to leave her alone for too long. I'd rather just pay extra so I can get home." Alex lied.

"Well ok, but you come back and see me in a few days and I'll remember this and get you what you need then. You're a good girl to worry after your Mom like that. I won't forget."

He gave her a nice smile and helped her pack up the canvas bags with groceries. Alex handed over the money, gave him a cheery wave and went to meet Cooper at the exit doors. She felt bad about lying to people but figured it was ok if it made things smoother on the road home. The exit doors were further down the building than the entrance doors and Alex was shocked to see a huge line up waiting to get in. Josh had moved the bikes to the far side of the parking lot away from the crowd and he was looking concerned. He was visibly relieved to see Alex and Cooper heading his way with carts of food

"Let's get this done fast and get out of here. I've already been approached twice about selling the bikes, and they weren't real happy to be told no." he said. After taking in the two carts he started shaking his head. "I don't think we can take all this guys."

Alex jumped in, "It's ok. A lot of this stuff can be taken out of the boxes and squished together." She told him.

They packed as much as they could into the three back backs and stuffed the saddle bags on the bikes close to bursting. They still had six bags of supplies that wouldn't fit and Josh started to go through them to see what would be discarded. Opening one of Cooper's bags he held up two cartons of cigarettes with a questioning look. "Last time I checked, none of us smoke, so are you planning to take up the habit dude?" he asked Cooper.

With a laugh Cooper answered, "No way man. Those are prime barter goods. People will be going crazy for them in the days ahead. We can trade them easily for stuff we need."

"That's good thinking but I don't know how we are going to take any more stuff. And what about these Alex, something you want to tell us? Who's the lucky guy?" he asked while holding up the condom boxes.

Alex felt her face go bright red in embarrassment. "Same thing, barter, and who knows maybe one of us might need them in the future. The far future." she stammered. "Anyways, I know how to take this stuff. Put all the rest into the canvas bags. I got some plastic zip ties we can attach the extra bags to our back packs until we get back to the trailers."

"Yeah, ok that will work, but we are seriously over loaded and off balance. It's going to be slow going till we get back to the others." Josh warned.

Alex and Josh got on their bikes and Cooper fastened the canvas bags to their packs with the zip ties. Alex realized right away how awkward it felt and tried to rebalance the bags. "This is going to be a rough ride." she sighed to herself.

Cooper had a soft sided insulated bag that was stuffed full and Alex wondered what was in it. He slung it over his neck so it rested on his chest. Alex laughed at how they looked, covered in packs and hanging bags but it quickly stopped being funny as they wobbled out of the parking lot and made their way out of town.

It took all of Alex's concentration to keep her bike upright and they were going very slowly. They had made it almost out of the business area when Alex rode past a mother pushing a stroller. She had biked ten feet past the stroller when what she heard penetrated her concentration.

"But Mommy, I'm hungry." wailed the child in the stroller.

"I know Baby, but I don't have any money and the bank machine isn't working. I'll find something at home to make." the mom tried to placate the child.

Alex came to a stop and quickly threw her feet out so her bike didn't tip over. She yelled at the boys to wait for her and they stopped and gave her concerned looks.

"It's ok, just give me a minute." she told them as she tried to balance her load and dug into her cargo pant pocket. The woman pushing the stroller was just coming even with her as she got the last of her money out of her pocket.

Alex turned to the woman, "Excuse me Ma'am, I couldn't help but overhear you. I just came from the grocery store myself and we got all we'll need. This is all the money I have left. Please take it and get back there." she said while pushing the money into her hand. "The line is crazy long so if you were turned away at the door, see if they will let you bypass it cause you already waited. Buy as much dried food as you can and then ration it. It might be awhile before there's any more brought in." she told the stunned woman.

"I can't take this. You don't even know me!" the woman protested, trying to hand the money back.

"You can take it, and you will! You have a hungry child to feed and that's the most important thing. You need to go back as fast as you can. Good luck!" Alex said as she got her bike going again.

She heard the woman yell after her, "Thank you Miss, you're an angel!"

Alex kept going and couldn't help but think of all the children that would be going hungry soon. She had tears rolling down her face by the time they made it the edge of town. Neither of the boys said anything to her but Josh gave her a sympathetic smile.

It took a lot longer to get back to Dara and Quinn than it had leaving them but they finally made it and staggered off their bikes and dropped their packs in exhaustion. Quinn and Dara went straight to the bags and started loading the trailers with the heavier goods and distributing the rest more evenly between back packs and the bike saddle bags. As they worked Dara noticed Alex's tear stained face and asked, "You ok Alex? Did something happen?"

Alex scrubbed at her face with her hands, "No it went really well. It just keeps hitting me how bad this is going to get for a lot of people." she sighed.

Cooper leaned toward her and tucked a curl behind her ear, "What you did for that family was really kind Alex. Yes, a lot of really bad things are going to happen to a lot of people in the next while but there will also be a lot of people who will come together and help each other too. You are a perfect example of that. Don't give up hope; we'll make it through this." he said, looking intensely into her eyes.

Alex could only nod and offer him a small smile of thanks. Something about Cooper kept her off balance and she didn't understand her feelings for him. She got up and brushed herself off; grabbing a water bottle and taking a long drink to cover her confusion. Quinn and Dara had repacked everything and Quinn gave her shoulder a comforting squeeze.

"You guys did great! This is way more than we thought you would get. Good idea with the zip ties. We can haul a lot more with these bags strapped to the trailers. If you guys have your breath back, let's head a couple more miles from town and find a better spot to stop and make some breakfast. I don't know about the rest of you but I'm starving." Quinn suggested.

Alex glanced at her watch and wasn't surprised to see that it was almost ten o'clock. The dried fruit and half a power bar she had eaten almost four hours ago was a distant memory and as a reminder her stomach gave a loud growl. They all mounted up and got back onto the main highway. It was an easier ride for her without the extra food weight and Quinn and Josh didn't seem to be bothered by the extra cargo on the trailers.

With everyone looking forward to a hot breakfast the group only biked for twenty minutes before pulling off on a side road and looking for an area to set up a camp. Five minutes off of the highway they wheeled off to an overgrown siding. Everyone got to work unloading camp stoves and fuel, plates and the camping cook set. When everything was set up they started to discuss what to make when Cooper took center stage. He had still been carrying the insulated cooler bag around his neck and when he opened it they were all delighted.

"I know we were supposed to get non-perishables and dry food but I couldn't resist. I figure it's going to be awhile before we have fresh food again and they had this stuff in with the frozen food so it's still good." he explained as he started pulling things out of the cooler.

The first thing out was a loaf of bread then a bunch of bananas. A box of frozen burgers was next, then a carton of eggs and a package of frozen breakfast sausage. Everyone was oohing and awing after each item. "So eggs and sausages for breakfast or brunch now, I guess and then burgers for later. They're still half frozen so they'll be thawed in time for supper. I did get some dry goods but I also grabbed a bag of apples and a small bag of potatoes to make things more appetizing." he finished with a flourish.

Everyone was excited about a real breakfast and no one complained a bit about Cooper straying from the list. Alex put a pot of water on the one stove to boil, adding five of the precious eggs to hard boil them for a later snack. She cut the sausages into small pieces and started to fry them up. Once they were nicely browned she cracked the rest of the eggs into the pan and scrambled them up with the sausage. Josh dug out the jar of peanut butter and once the pan of eggs and sausage came off the stove, started to toast part of the loaf of bread. Once everyone had a plate of food they settled on the tarp that Quinn had spread out. There was no talking as they consumed the first real meal that they had had in over twenty four hours.

Cooper and Dara cleaned up the dishes and cookware while Alex and Josh repacked the gear into the trailers.

Quinn was looking at the map with a frown on his face. "Well it was sooo worth it, but so far today we've only made about twenty miles. What do you guys say to going hard until about seven tonight with just a quick stop for a snack? If we push it we could make it another sixty or seventy miles." That was met by a chorus of groans but after a full breakfast, they were all agreeable.

Chapter 8

Six hours later and Alex didn't even have the energy to moan. She didn't know what was worse, the boredom of mile after mile of scrub landscape or the total exhaustion she was feeling. Hot and sweaty, her face felt like it would crack if she tried to smile, it was so dry from the sun and wind. She tried to console herself with the thought of the great muscle tone she would have, but it didn't feel that way at the moment.

A couple of hours after they had started this leg of the journey they had come upon an interesting sight. For a good five miles, every car they passed had its doors and the trunk standing open. It made navigating the wrecks more difficult but did change the dynamic of the ride for a half hour. Alex hoped that whoever had searched all the cars found what they needed. They had also started seeing more people walking alone or in small groups. They had no issues with the other travellers, just envious stares. Quinn had pulled them over when one family had waved them down.

Three children and their parents, looking dusty and tired, were travelling in the opposite direction and the father had waved them down with a shout for news. As the group explained what they had seen on the way to this point, Cooper handed out granola bars and a couple apples to the children. Those were devoured in minutes and the mother couldn't stop thanking him. They seemed like a nice family and after a quick group conference they agreed to give them a gallon jug of water and a few packages of freeze dried camping meals. Dara pulled out the sunscreen and asked the mother if she wanted to coat the children up with the lotion. As they pulled away, it seemed like such a small thing they had done, helping the family but it made biking past all the destruction a little easier.

Other than a few quick bathroom breaks on the side of the road and one short stop to eat, they had been making steady progress. Lunch was hardboiled eggs and the bananas that Cooper had provided, but Alex was still feeling hungry. She wondered how many calories she was burning a day biking like this and amused herself by coming up with different diet titles like, "The Apocalypse Bike Diet". She had thought she was in shape with all of her gymnastic training but her body was suffering like she was a couch potato. Only the second day of the disaster and she was already dreaming of Big Macs and French fries. Her mouth was watering at the thought of the fast food meal when Josh gave a "Whoa" of alarm.

They came to a quick stop and looked down the road to what was blocking the highway. Alex took advantage of the break to remove her bike helmet and vigorously scratch at her sweaty, itchy scalp. Two days of dust and sweat with no shower and her dirty hair was driving her nuts.

Further down the road, someone had pushed abandoned cars across the highway to make a barrier. Alex could see at least three men with shotguns or rifles standing behind the road block. One of the men waved them forward and Quinn waved back turning to the group.

"Okay, let's stay cool and see what the deal is but be ready if they try anything."

As they pedaled closer to the road block, the man that had waved them forward came out to meet them.

"Hey there folks, we're getting a lot of travellers coming in to town and we've set things up to greet them and get news and check on their intentions." He looked them over, his face softening a bit seeing how young they all were. "Where are you kids coming from and where are you headed?" he asked. The other two men had come closer to hear their answer.

Quinn answered for the group, "We were at Disneyland when the lights went out and we are trying to make it home."

The man was clearly surprised by this. "Disneyland? That's over a hundred miles from here. You guys biked all that way in two days?" he asked skeptically. He looked at the other men in disbelief.

"Yes sir, we had a teacher who got us moving right away. She got us organized and on the road within an hour. We used all the spending money we had to buy these bikes and we've been going hard ever since." Quinn assured him.

The man let out a whistle of surprise, "Woo hoo, you kids should be mighty thankful to that teacher. She probably saved all your lives. I imagine the city is a cesspool of violence by now. So where is this teacher and the rest of your class?"

Quinn looked sad as he told the man, "Part of our group headed for the coast to try and get a boat out. Our teacher, Mrs. Moore stayed with the rest, who wanted to wait for help to come. She wouldn't leave them."

The man shook his head in disgust, "Damn sheep. What a waste of a good woman and teacher." He paused to think, "A boat? Where are you kids going, where's home?"

"Canada." several of the kids replied.

All the men broke out in surprised laughter but stopped when they realized that the kids were serious.

"Listen, you kids can't be serious. Do you really think you can bike all the way to Canada?" one of the men challenged them.

None of the group responded, just stared back at the men with determination. After studying their faces, the leader of the roadblock shook his head, "Well, you just never know. You might make it. In the meantime, it's getting late so if you kids want, you're welcome to stay in town tonight. We've set up a hotel as a refugee area and there's room and a meal for you." He waved toward town.

"Thank you sir for the offer, but we plan on going another hour down the road today and then setting up camp for the night. We're trying to make as many miles as we can every day." Quinn said with a smile. "We would appreciate any water that you could spare though. We're down a couple of bottles. We gave some of our supply to a family with children that were walking."

"Now I know you kids was raised right! Are you sure you don't want to stay in our town? We will need good people in the coming days." he asked again.

They all said thank you but no.

"Alright, fair enough, I'd want to try for home too. John, ride back into town with these kids and help them top of their water. Give them two extra jugs as well." he instructed one of his men. "What about food, do you have enough food?" he asked eyeing the two trailers they pulled. "We don't have a lot of extra in town but I'm sure we could give you a day or two worth."

"Thank you Sir, that's a very kind and generous offer but we stopped first thing this morning at a town and spent the rest of our money stocking up. We're good to go for about a week or so. Please save the food for people who really need it." Alex jumped in.

"Alright then, good luck finding your way north and be real careful. This is the calm before the storm and I think it's going to be a bad one." He waved them through and they biked around the road block.

John, the man that they followed into town was driving an old beat up golf cart. Josh pedaled up beside him and pointed at the engine, "Carburetor?" he asked.

John gave him an appraising look. "Yup, seems most older engines that don't have a lot of electronics will still work."

Josh gave a nod and fell back with the others. As they came into the town, they could see that there had been work done to clean up the main road. All the useless vehicles had been moved off to the side and there were guards with guns walking in front of the businesses. They pulled into a parking lot and came to a halt. Pulling out their two empty jugs from one of the trailers, they passed them to John and he took them in to the building. It wasn't long before he came back out with another man, both carrying two jugs each.

They handed them over and John asked, "Do you kids know what's ahead of you? It's just over sixty miles to the town of Baker. After that it's going to be a hard bike upwards. The elevation goes up double from where we're standing to Mountain Pass before it goes back down and you head into real desert. You couldn't pay me to go anywhere near Vegas, it'll be even worse than LA. It's going to be a real bitch of a trip. I wouldn't do it on a bike but I guess I understand your reasons. It's going to be dark in just over an hour so you better get a move on. Good luck to you."

They said their thanks and got back on the highway that went through town. They were all quiet and thoughtful about what was ahead of them. Alex just wanted to stop for the night and eat and sleep. She could worry about the way ahead tomorrow. It took a lot of effort to get back up to speed after stopping in the town but once they cleared the last of it, they fell into the rhythm of navigating around stalled cars and started to make better time. Alex was so consumed with exhaustion and hunger that she was jolted out of her fog by Quinn calling out to her. She hadn't even heard him the first time

"Hey, I said we're taking this side road to find a place to set up camp. You look wiped out Alex. Let's go find home for the night." He told her with a concerned smile.

Alex took in their surroundings and noticed the sign for the road they were turning down Ghost Road. Perfect, that's exactly how she felt, like a ghost. The sun was going down and the shadows were long when they came to a trail with an old shed and rusted out pump jack in a clearing.

Wheeling into it and dropping their packs, Alex stood still, numb and dazed. She wondered if a person could fall asleep standing up. Dara dragged an old plastic milk crate over and gently pushed Alex down onto it. She handed her a water bottle and an apple.

"Just eat this and sip some water. We'll get the tents set up and the stove going. Relax and get your breath back." Dara told her.

Alex nibbled on the apple but was still out of it. She vaguely heard the others talking as they set up camp and she thought she heard someone say something about her being in shock. Shock seemed like a good word to her, that's how she felt, like someone had shocked her and she was in slow motion. She didn't know how long she sat on the crate but at some point Dara took away the apple and made her take two Advil.

It was the sound and smell of a fire that snapped her out of the fog she was in. Slowly things started making sense to Alex again and she saw Quinn busting up old wooden boards for the small camp fire they had going. Dara was unrolling sleeping bags and laying them out in the tents while Josh and Cooper were arguing about potatoes. It took a minute for that to make sense but then she understood what they were talking about. Josh wanted to just put the whole potato into the fire and Cooper wanted to fry them somehow.

"Foil," Alex croaked at them. The whole camp came to a stop and stared at her in confusion and concern. She tried again, "Foil, cut the potatoes up and put them in foil with a little water. I got cooking spray."

It took a minute but they finally understood she was back and not just talking nonsense. Cooper gave her an encouraging smile and Quinn just nodded to her. Dara came over and squatted down in front of her, looking at her face.

"You look better, Alex. Some color is back in your face and your eyes aren't glazed anymore. You had us worried. When we stopped you were as white as a sheet and you were shaking. I think you were going into shock. Too much crazy, huh?"

"Yeah, I guess, just kinda lost it there for a minute." she joked.

"More like twenty minutes." Dara told her. "I don't think we're going to be able to keep going like this, at least not this hard every day."

She patted Alex's knee and went back to the tents. Alex went over to Cooper to see if she could help with making supper. He had found the foil and was cutting up the potatoes.

"Sorry about that, had to go visit la la land for awhile. Why don't you let me take over for you? I make a mean foil potato surprise. I've got a secret recipe that I use." she joked.

He looked into her eyes intensely and grabbed her hand, "Okay, but no more trips, at least not without me. You scared the hell out me Alex. We need you here with us."

If Alex hadn't been in shock before, she definitely was now. She felt her cheeks flame up and mumbled a quick, "Sorry." She looked down and grabbed the box of foil and started to make a pouch for the potatoes.

She didn't understand the feelings she had for Cooper. She could feel him staring at her for a few minutes before he turned away. Once she was alone she looked up and did a quick scan of the others to see if anyone had witnessed the exchange and met Quinn's gaze. He was standing with an old board forgotten in his hand and a frown on his face. He had clearly seen the moment between her and Cooper and he wasn't happy about it.

This was more than Alex's tired brain could deal with and she quickly turned away. This isn't the time to deal with boy issues she thought and stuffed her confusion down deep. Eventually it would all surface, but right now making supper was all she could handle.

She went to one of the trailers and rummaged around, looking for the rest of the supplies she needed. After going through both of the trailers she had finally found everything. The light was almost gone and Alex reminded herself to pull everything out in the morning and organize and repack everything.

First she sprayed the inside of her foil pouch with the cooking spray she had bought and added the potatoes. A small can of corn was added and a dose of dried mixed spices sprinkled on top. She folded the pouch closed except for one end and added a small amount of water. After sealing the pouch she gave it a good shake and placed it on the foldable grill that Josh had set up over the camp fire. Looking around for something to do while the food cooked, Alex saw that Dara had a steaming pot of water going on one of the camp stoves. Alex remembered seeing a sleeve of disposable coffee cups when she was pulling food out of the trailer and guessed it was another Cooper addition. They wouldn't have to share coffee mugs tonight. After getting the cups and drink mixes like instant coffee and powdered hot chocolate, she flipped the vegetable pouch and grabbed the canvas bag full of toiletries. The tent that Dara had set up for them was open and she was sorting things out when Alex crawled in.

"Hey, I didn't have a chance to show you some of the stuff I got for us at the store this morning." Alex told her. She dumped the bag of supplies out on a sleeping bag and Dara whooped in pleasure.

"Deodorant! I could kiss you right now Alex." she exclaimed with pleasure while sorting through the rest of the goods. "Oh, shampoo! What I wouldn't give to wash my hair. It feels like ants are crawling through it, it's so itchy." Grabbing the hair dye kit, she studied the shade, "This will work. Good choice. It's almost my natural color so I won't have to worry about root growth." She laughed. Setting the box aside she kept looking through the stuff and made a disgusted face, "Oh man, how much is it going to suck having our periods while biking all day. Thank God you grabbed tampons. Can you imagine if we didn't have any; what a disaster that would've been." Surveying the rest she leaned back, "Everything we need except a hot shower." She sighed. "After we eat, we should try and wash out some of our shirts. They're pretty ripe. Hopefully they will be close to dry by morning. And could you color my hair for me? Those guys at the road block today were definitely giving my blue streaks "the look". No sense borrowing trouble. I don't even care about the color. I only did it to try and piss off my parents and I don't think they even noticed!" she said in a huff.

Alex was surprised by the admission. She didn't know what Dara's home life was like since she had stopped hanging out with them a few years ago but she remembered Dara's Mom and Dad as being nice people. She started to ask about it when the smell of hamburgers came through the tent opening and Josh called out, "Grub's ready!" Dara quickly left the tent with an embarrassed expression on her face, so Alex didn't think she wanted to talk about it. Alex realized that she didn't know anything about Dara's life now and decided that they would get to know each other better on the long trip home.

They filled their camping plates with spiced, steamy potatoes, corn and the hamburger patties on the last of the toasted bread. Two hot meals in one day would seem like heaven in the days to come and they all focused on enjoying the meal.

Once they all had cups of hot drinks, Dara filled the pot to boil more water for the cleanup. They settled around the low fire and discussed the next day.

Quinn started with, "Even stopping for a few hours today, we made a lot of miles. But I don't think we can keep up that kind of pace every day. Especially with what's ahead. I don't know about Josh but hauling the trailers on flat ground isn't that bad. Hauling them up hill will be killer. And we'll all suffer once we hit the desert. I think we'll have to slow down. That guy John is right about Las Vegas. All those tourists on top of the city population, it's going to be a mad house. I think we should start looking for back roads to get around it. We might even have to go overland." He paused thoughtfully. "I wish we knew the area better. If it was home, between all of our knowledge, we could come up with ten different ways to avoid town." he sighed. "I wish we had grabbed some binoculars at the camping store. They would really come in handy to scout ahead."

Cooper brought up a scary topic, "I think today and tomorrow will be the last of the goodwill from people. Two days without water flowing and no help arriving and they'll start thinking clearer. No food shipments, no transport, tomorrow is when things are going to really start breaking down. The worst of society will start taking

~ 77 ~

advantage of things and we might be biking into trouble anytime we get near towns. We really will have to stay alert for ambushes and be prepared to defend ourselves. What we have in those trailers could be worth our lives to some people."

Josh agreed, "We all have to be ready. Alex, Dara, if someone is going to try and hurt us you have to be prepared to defend us. My Dad always told my sister, "One of the most dangerous things is a gun in the hands of a woman who won`t use it". People, especially bad people can tell when you don`t really mean it. So you two really have to mean it. Don`t hesitate. All our lives will be at stake."

Dara`s attitude flared up, "Yeah, thanks for the pep talk but try to remember who my Dad is. I`m a cop`s daughter. He fed me, "Shoot for the center mass" with my wheaties. I won`t have a problem and let`s not forget Alex`s brother is a cop as well. I have complete faith in her judgement. How about you Josh, are you going to scare them away with a cherry bomb?" she asked sarcastically.

"Hey that's not fair! I might like to do pranks but in case you haven't noticed, none of us are screwing around. We all want to get home safely. I mean look at you, changing your hair so you won't stand out. Sooo not the Dara I know. Alex has barely said two words since yesterday and usually you can't get a word in edgewise with her. Have you seen Cooper steal a car yet? And Quinn…Ok Quinn's still Mr. Responsibility. But all that stuff is over. The faces we showed to everyone a few days ago? They weren't the real us, it was just a way to get through the day. This is who we really are, people who will help others when we can and defend ourselves against the bad when we have to. So yeah, I might like to chuck cherry bombs in garbage cans at school, but here on the road, I will kill someone to keep you safe." he said forcefully and with meaning.

Everyone was shocked a little by his outburst and before anyone could respond he jumped up and walked away.

Trying to reduce the tension Cooper yelled after him, "Hey, I would gladly steal a car for you buddy!" they heard a half laugh, half sob as he kept going.

After a few minutes of silence, Dara got up and walked out to meet him in the dark. Josh had always been like a brother to Alex, and after what he just said; she realized that she would do anything to keep him safe as well. They were all trying to deal with this new situation and Alex understood that they were all shaking off their high school personalities and becoming adults.

"Well, Mr. Responsibility says let's get this place cleaned up and hit the sack." Quinn tried to joke but it came out flat.

With the help of the lantern, they cleaned up the dishes and Alex collected dirty shirts to wash. She didn't know how well they would wash but it would be an improvement from the sweaty, stinky mess they currently were. After swishing them one by one through the hot water with a couple drops of dish soap she rung them out and draped them over the bikes and trailers to dry. Dara and Josh were still out in the dark together so Alex went to the tent and grabbed some of the toiletries and handed them out to Quinn and Cooper. A bag of baby wipes in hand, she closed the tent flap and tried to wash off the day's grime. It felt like heaven to be partially clean and she really didn't want to put her dirty clothes back on. She was worried about space when she grabbed clothes from the sports store, so all she had grabbed other than socks and underwear was a spare outfit. A pair of shorts and yoga pants, an extra shirt and a jacket that could be rolled up was all she had extra. The shirt she had just removed was dirty and the other one was air drying so she pulled on the jacket, which had a nice cozy fleece lining. After wearing her cargo pants for two days, they could almost stand up by themselves so she grabbed the yoga pants and shimmied into them. Fresh socks helped cushion her feet. After that she tackled her hair. The normally bouncy, strawberry blond curls were dirty and matted. Brushing it ruthlessly, she got all the tangles and knots out and it did seem to help her scalp feel less itchy. Feeling almost normal, she put her boots back on and headed back out of the tent.

Dara and Josh had come back while she was getting cleaned up and as Alex walked past him, she lightly bumped shoulders and gave him a wink. "Just so you know how much you mean to me, I'll wash out your dirty clothes if you hand them over." she joked with him.

With an evil grin, the old Josh surfaced, "Aw, thanks Alex, I'll go grab you my dirty underwear!"

"Nice try. I don't love you that much! Give me your shorts and shirt, you fool!" she laughed.

She had put yet another pot of water on to heat after she had done the first bunch of shirts and she was getting worried about their water supply again. Even with the two extra jugs that they had got at the last town, they would have to find more every day. Dara was cleaning herself up in the tent while Alex finished washing the extra clothes and she passed out her dirty clothes with the promise to take on the next night's laundry duty. By the time she had hung up the last shirt to dry, her hands were aching from the hot water and ringing them all out. She couldn't help but think of all the simple things they used to take for granted. Turn the washer on and walk away, voila! Clean clothes. Turn the microwave on and walk away, instant hot food. Everything was so much work now - but the worst was the dead piece of plastic she had left back in the sports store. Not being able to instantly talk to her parents or friends was killing her. The total uncertainty of what was happening at home was so hard. With a sigh, she tilted her watch to the lanterns light and saw it was just after eight. She had to laugh at herself for wanting to go to bed. Most nights it was close to midnight before she would go to sleep and for the last two nights she was out by nine.

Alex scanned their camp site and saw everything was put away so she joined the boys at the burned down campfire. They were working out the nights guard schedule. Alex and Dara had not taken a turn at the motel so she offered to stand a watch tonight.

"Thanks Alex, but last night doesn't really count. Except for Quinn who had to wake up in the middle of the night it was pretty easy sitting in that room. So we decided that Josh will go first until midnight and then he'll wake me up and I'll wake Quinn at three." Cooper told her just as Dara joined them.

She disagreed right away. "I'll take the last watch so Quinn gets a full night sleep. It's really sweet that you guys are trying to let us off watch but don't forget, you and Josh are pulling the trailers, Quinn. You need rest. Alex needs tonight off but she will be ready to take her turn tomorrow night. Right Alex?"

"You bet. I'm sure I could stand a watch tonight. I'm sorry about earlier but I feel much better now."

Everyone shook their heads at that so she agreed that she would take her turn the next night.

"One more thing before we turn in guys." Quinn advised, "We need to put out the fire and keep the lantern off. It's like a beacon to anyone out there, advertising that we're here and the light would ruin any night vision, making it harder for us to see anything coming our way. So keep the lantern close but keep it off unless you need it. Don't take any chances, if you think someone's coming, wake us up, better safe than sorry."

Alex shivered, thinking about sitting out here all alone in the dark. From all the camping she had done at home, she knew that outside sounds in the night could be scary. Crawling into her sleeping bag was so sweet, for about two minutes, then all the grounds bumps were felt in her sore muscles. Her last thought before sleep took her was that they would need to find more toilet paper.

Chapter 9

Alex was dreaming. She was in her comfy bed at home and could hear her Mother rattling dishes while making breakfast. She could smell coffee and their dog, Dawson was barking.

"Mom, let the dog out!" she called, and it was the sound of her own voice that woke her. She had called out in her sleep. She tried to go back to sleep, to that warm feeling of being in her own bed but the dog was still barking. Opening her eyes and staring up at the roof of the tent she was jolted by how bright it was. She scrambled for her watch and saw it was after seven. Doing the math, she realized that she had slept for more than ten hours. "Wow, I must have really needed that." she thought.

Crawling out of the sleeping bag, putting on her boots and wondering why no one had woken her, it was as she went to unzip the tent flap that she saw Dara sleeping. Oh no, Dara was supposed to be on watch. Debating on whether to wake her or not, she heard someone cough outside and decided to go out first. As quietly as possible she let herself out of the tent and zipped it back up. Quinn was the only one up and out, so she went over to see what was going on. He had both of the trailers and all the saddle bags emptied out and was organizing their supplies.

"Good morning." she greeted him, "I was going to do that this morning. Try to make it easier to find the stuff we need when we stop. Isn't it kind of late? What happened to Dara taking the last watch?" she asked.

"Good morning to you too." he smiled, handing her his coffee to share. "I woke up at five thirty and couldn't get back to sleep, so I took over from her and she went back to bed. I thought we would have a later start today. Our bodies need time to adjust to all this biking." The barking dog started up again and he turned to look that way.

"I didn't notice any houses nearby last night, did you?" Alex asked him.

"No and I still can't see any. It's coming from further down this road." he frowned. There was an almost frantic tone to the barking and then it fell silent again.

Turning back to the piles of supplies, Alex was strangely pleased to see they had a six pack of toilet paper. Shrugging her shoulders she started to organize with Quinn. She was happy to see all the things that Cooper had gotten at the store that would make things easier. When Quinn unearthed the cartons of cigarettes and condoms, Alex was quick to explain Cooper's barter idea.

"He's smart. I'm glad he's with us. He thinks of things that the rest of us wouldn't. It's a real asset." And then out of the blue, "Do you like him?" Quinn asked with penetrating blue eyes.

Alex was immediately flustered. "Sure, I mean yeah, he's a great guy. I mean, it's good he's with us to help along the way. I'm going to make more coffee." She stammered out and went to rush away to the stove, almost tripping over a pile of tarps.

When she got to the stove, she forced herself to take a deep breath and calm down. She knew Quinn was still looking at her, unsatisfied with her answer. She wasn't ready to think about Cooper that way, let alone talk to Quinn about it. She and Quinn had always had an underlining tension to their relationship. They often paired up on projects and in group situations but it had never developed into more than friendship. Alex shook her head in disbelief.

"The end of the world as we know it and I'm having boy problems," she thought. "Really?"

Alex started to check on all the clothes she had hung up to dry last night and was happy that most were only damp around the seams. Her cargo pants were the worst, so she laid them out in a patch of sunlight and hoped for the best. The others started to emerge from their tents so she got busy making pancake mix up and decided to make a double batch so she could add ham to it for a lunch version. They could pack it to go in one of the disposable containers she had bought and it would make a ready lunch later on. As the first few cooked in the camp pan, she cut up the canned ham for the later batch. Every now and then she lifted her head, looking in the direction the barking seemed to be coming from. Dishing up the first few plates, she noticed the others often looking that way as well.

After everyone had eaten, Cooper cleaned the pans, Josh started to take the tents down and Dara, Alex and Quinn packed up and reorganized supplies into the trailers and saddlebags. They worked it out so everyone's backpacks had their own personal supplies like extra clothes and toiletries as well as a small amount of dry food and water.

As they were putting their packs on and getting ready to head back to the highway, the barking changed to a mournful howl that Alex felt pierce her heart. It was the saddest sound. They got on their bikes and wheeled out to the side road that would take them back to the highway. Alex was in the lead and she came to a stop, looking in the direction they were meant to go, and then slowly looked the other way in the direction of the sad howling.

Everyone was looking at her expectantly. "I don't know." she said. "It feels like we should check, like we're meant to check. I don't know." She frowned, feeling uncertain. "Something makes me feel like we have to. Do you guys understand?"

It was Cooper that broke the silence. "I always try and go with my gut feeling, so if yours is telling you we should go, then we should." He looked to the rest for confirmation and they all nodded agreement.

"Okay, let's go check on the sad dog but everyone be ready for trouble just in case." Quinn warned.

So the group headed away from the highway and further down Ghost Road. It didn't take long before they came over a rise and saw a square of trees planted around a house with a couple of out buildings. There was a driveway with an open gate set ten feet off the road. It was hard to see the property with the trees surrounding it, but as they came even with the driveway a Golden Retriever raced toward them. It stopped at the gate and started to bark and whine at them, doing the classic doggy 'follow me' dance at them and then turn back with an 'are you coming' look over its shoulder.

Josh joked, "Do you think its name is Lassie and Timmy's in the well?"

"Ha ha, very funny Josh," Alex said sarcastically, "It definitely wants us to follow, so let's go see." she said as she started slowly down the driveway.

The dog took off ahead and cut towards the house across the lawn. As they got closer they could see it was standing, barking at them from beside a bush with flowers on it. There was a mound of dirt with a shovel sticking out of it and the dog was standing over a crumpled form of a man lying on the ground. Without hesitating, Alex dumped her bike and rushed toward the man. The dog's whine changed to a growl and Alex dropped to her knees a few feet away at the warning.

"Oh, poor puppy, I'm so sorry. Its ok, it's ok now. We'll help. Come here baby." Alex cooed to the dog and held out her hands in a non-threatening way. At the tone, the dog went to its belly and slid closer to her. Once it was close enough, the dog sniffed at her hands and with a whine, nudged under them so she could rub its head. Keeping up a steady stream of nonsensical baby talk, the dog was soon her best friend, and with a wagging tail moved over so she could check on the man. Staying on her knees to keep the dog calm, she reached for the man and checked for a pulse.

"Good dog, what a good boy." she told him as she felt the dog stiffen as she reached for his owner. He settled his body along the man and rested his head on the man's chest, whining softly.

Alex guessed the man was in his sixties or early seventies. He had a weak pulse and was breathing shallowly. Alex smoothed back his white hair and felt his skin to be very dry. She dumped her backpack off and grabbed a water bottle and wash cloth out of it. Wetting the cloth she wiped the man's face down and squeezed a few drops into his mouth. The water seemed to bring him around some and he let out a groan so she squeezed more water out for him. The dog lifted his head and gave a half-hearted growl at something behind Alex. The man's hand came up and rested it on the dogs back calming it as his eyes fluttered open. When he seemed to focus on Alex, she gave him a reassuring smile.

"Hi, looks like you took a little fall here. Can you handle some water?" she said brightly to keep him calm. He nodded, so Alex held the water bottle to his lips, "Not too much. Let's save the heavy drinking for when you're back on your feet." she joked. Alex had volunteered at the senior's home in her town and knew that fear and confusion was the first thing a person feels when they become aware after waking. She kept her tone light and fun so the man would know he was safe.

As he took sips from the bottle, she kept talking, "My name is Alex and your beautiful dog persuaded me and my friends to come and help you." When he made an attempt to sit up she braced herself behind him to help. "I'd like to get you out of the sun. Is it ok if some of my friends help?" The man looked past her to the group that was standing off to the side. They hadn't wanted to upset the dog so they stayed back. He nodded again so Alex turned to her friends, "Cooper can you grab a patio chair and put it into the shade, please? Josh, Quinn, will you help him into it?"

The dog started growling again as the boys approached and the man spoke for the first time, "Down boy, friends." he commanded in a gruff voice. The dog instantly relaxed and started to wag his tail

With the boys on either side of the man, Alex backed out of the way and they guided him to the chair Cooper had retrieved. Now that the man had reassured the dog, it was busy running from person to person, sniffing them and getting petted. Alex looked around the lawn and realized what the mound of dirt was. She stepped closer and peered down into the hole beside it. A body wrapped in a white sheet lay at the bottom, waiting to be covered. She turned back to the man with a look of sadness. He was staring at the open grave, clutching the water bottle.

"My wife, she died yesterday." he explained. "She was diabetic and had a fancy insulin pump. It stopped working with everything else. I walked to our neighbor's house, four miles down the road, but they are away in Florida, visiting their son. I remembered Tom has an old 1950's, restored farm truck and gave it a shot. Started up on the first try, but by the time I got back June had already passed. She loved those Oleander bushes, so that's where I was going to lay her to rest. Started at first light this morning, to beat the heat and got her down in there but when I climbed out I felt dizzy. Next thing I know, I'm lookin' up at your pretty red hair." he said weakly, his energy spent. He slumped to the side, barely staying in his chair.

Quinn helped straighten him up, "Sir, please let us help you finish that." he solemnly told the man.

"Thank you son, it'll keep for a minute. Let's just sit a spell and you kids tell me how you ended up here. Alex, you said your name is? Could you go in the house, there's a pitcher of sweet tea on the kitchen table. Bring out some glasses and we'll all have tea while I get my strength back and hear your story."

"Yes of course. I'll be right back." she said and with Dara in tow walked around the house to the front door.

The front driveway had been expanded for parking and there was a strange assortment of new and old vehicles parked there. A huge new motor home sat beside the garage with a newer truck parked in the garage. On the other side was an older, smaller Winnebago motor home camper. Parked in front of the house was an antique forest green farm truck with wooden side boards enclosing the truck bed. It was shiny and looked well cared for. Alex could see a small barn further back on the property and she could hear the clucking of chickens and mooing of cows.

Beside the front door was a welcome sign that read, Welcome to the Peterson's, Luke and June. The girls entered the dim farm house and walked back into the kitchen. Dara collected glasses for all of them and Alex carried the pitcher of tea back out. As they came back around the corner they heard Quinn telling Mr. Peterson about their trip so far and how they were going to keep heading north to Canada. Dara started pouring tea for everyone and passed Alex a glass to hand to Mr. Peterson. His hand shook as he reached for it and Alex had to steady it for him. Looking into his face she could see he wasn't doing very well. His skin had an unhealthy grey pallor to it.

"Sir, do you have any family nearby that could come and stay to help you?" she asked. They couldn't leave this man alone in his poor condition.

With a resigned smile he shook his head. "It's just me and June here now. Both our boys live on the East coast. No one will be coming, besides, I don`t think I'll be here much longer and to be honest, with my Juney gone I don't really want to stay." When Alex tried to disagree he waved her silent. "So let's talk turkey." his voice getting firmer, "Your friend filled me in on where you been and where you're going. You seem like good kids and if it was my boys stuck far from home I'd want someone to help them. Biking all the way up to Canada is just plain crazy, even being young and full of get up. So you'll load up those bikes and take Tom's old truck. As a matter of fact, I never even thought to try the old camper. It's an early seventies model so it just might work. I've kept it serviced and put new tires on it a few years back. I don't know why we kept it after we bought that huge road hog. Lots of good memories I guess. Anyways, there's extra gas cans in the shed so you can siphon out the gas from the new truck and big motor home. They won't be going anywhere so they don't need the gas. You girls can get all the extra food we have put up in the basement. Take as much as you can fit and there will still be plenty left for me. I'll just ask that you help me put June to rest and you should be on your way."

The life seemed to drain out of him as he finished what would be his last will and testament. The drinking glass slid from his hand and dropped to the grass. The dog let out a heartbreaking howl and Alex didn't need to check his pulse to know he had gone to join his Juney.

No one moved or spoke for a while, just sitting and absorbing what had just happened. It was Josh who finally stood and when Alex looked to him she saw tears streaming down his face. He walked to the hole in the ground and in a raw voice asked, "Some help here guys?" and dropped down into the hole. "Let's take her out and widen it so they can lie together."

Cooper dropped in and it was with the greatest respect that Quinn, Dara and Alex took the body and carried it over to lie beside Mr. Peterson's chair. The boys took turns digging the hole wider and the girls went back into the house for a bed sheet. They got the man down and had him wrapped in the sheet by the time the grave was ready. After placing the bodies side by side, they filled the grave and stood around it in silence.

Alex dropped to her knees and placed her hand on the loose soil, "Thank you Mr. Peterson, please thank your wife for us." and she rose and walked away. The others followed suit all kneeling and thanking the man that had provided the way home for them.

** ** ** ** ** **

Alex sat on a tree swing lost in thought. She couldn't bear to go into the house so soon after Mr. Peterson's death. She was thinking about his sons and wondering if they were feeling like she was. Wondering if their parents were okay and trying to get home to them. What if strangers had had to bury her parents? The not knowing was the worst feeling Alex had ever known. Hearing Josh curse loudly brought her out of her gloomy thoughts and she saw the boys were still working on the engine of the old camper. Dara came out of the house and headed her way. She settled on the grass close by but didn't say anything. After a few minutes she began talking.

"I believe that there is a reason for everything. I believe there is more than just our existence, our everyday life. I don't know if it's God or Fate or even Mother Earth, but I believe there is something that plays its hand in what we do and the choices we make. This morning, we were headed to the desert and possibly our deaths. Something told you to turn the other way, something that will now change our odds of getting home. That man woke up and saw nothing but kindness in your face and he returned it. Take that gift and honour it, use it and repay it when you can. Let's go home Alex." With that she got up and walked away.

Alex looked over at the fresh grave where the dog still lay. She was saddened that she didn't even know its name. She thought about Dara's words and resolved to keep looking forward, to the way home. She gave a huge push to the swing and pumped her legs to get higher, finally doing a flying dismount and used the momentum to keep going.

She was almost at the old camper when she heard its engine turn over. The boys gave a huge cheer and Alex couldn't contain the grin on her face. Two vehicles to get them home meant double the chance of making it.

"Josh, you're amazing!" she congratulated him.

"No problem. I just had to rework some stuff and presto! Wheels!" He said modestly. "This is going to be great. We can fill the holding tanks with water so we don't have to lug the jugs around and we should have a working propane stove and fridge. No more roughing it for us. This old girl sleeps six, so we won't have to sleep on the ground."

Quinn was beaming, "This is going to make all the difference. We won't be killing ourselves everyday biking and we can carry more supplies. With all the wrecked cars on the roads, we can get all the gas we need. Even if we have to leave one, we will still have another to keep going in. We just cut the time it'll take us to get home by weeks." he said excitedly with a big smile.

Alex had never seen him so excited. She wondered how hard the disaster must have been weighing on him. Her and Josh had both vented some of the pressure but so far the others had kept it together.

"We should stay here for today and sort out supplies and load everything up. I want to strap the bikes onto the roof just in case and we have other things to do that will take a while. Let's just stay here and work at it, then leave first thing tomorrow." Quinn suggested.

Everyone agreed, so Alex headed to the house to help Dara sort out supplies and fill her in. The house was heating up as the day progressed, so Alex went around opening all the windows to air it out. Hearing noises from the basement she headed down looking for Dara.

The basement was cooler than the upstairs and very dim. She could see light off at the end so she made her way around the outline of a coffee table, passing a TV and an arm chair. Just as she was going to pass into the next room, something caught her eye. Moving closer to try and make it out in the dim light, she realized what it was. A gun safe was against one wall and it was the same type that her Dad kept his hunting rifles in. Reminding herself to look for keys to it later she turned to go in to the next room when she heard a soft sob. Freezing at the sound, she could make out Dara`s quiet crying in the next room. Debating on giving her privacy, Alex remembered Dara holding her hand in a dark hotel room and entered the room. A lantern burned in the center of the room, illuminating a storage area with metal shelves filled with canning jars and dried goods. Dara was sitting on the floor with her knees up against her chest and her arms wrapped tightly around them. She was crying softly and rocking back and forth.

Alex walked up behind her, kneeled down and wrapped her arms around her. At first Dara stiffened but then collapsed back into Alex`s arms, dissolving into heartbreaking sobs. Alex didn`t say anything, just held the girl and let her cry it out. After a while she calmed and started to sniff. Alex spotted a case of tissues on the shelf and got up to open the case, passing a box to her. Dara mopped her face, blew her nose and took a deep breath.

"I'm sorry, Alex. It just overwhelmed me. I can't stop worrying about Jake. Who's taking care of Jake?" she finished on a sob.

Alex was confused. She knew Jake was Dara's little brother. He had been just a toddler when they had moved into town and Alex guessed he was around seven or eight. She was confused because she expected that Dara's mother would be looking after him.

"I'm sure your Mom will take care of him. They'll be all right." Alex tried to console.

Dara started to laugh and it wasn't a nice laugh but a bitter one. "My Mom? Oh yeah, I'm sure as soon as she sobers up she'll be the best protector for him." she said sarcastically. "My Mom's a drunk, Alex, has been since my Dad left. I take care of Jake." she looked down with shame.

"But, but, why didn't you tell us? We could have helped you. We were your best friends." Alex said in shock.

Dara shook her head, "At first I was ashamed and didn't want anyone to know. I thought she would get better. After a while, I was so angry, so mad at the world. I even hated you and Emily because you still had a real family. I was so busy cleaning up my Mom's mess and trying to take care of Jake that I just let everything else go. It was easier if I didn't have to talk about it so I just stayed away from you guys. The only one I couldn't shake was Josh. He just kept coming around, sitting with me no matter what I said to him, he always came back. He figured out what was going on with my Mom pretty quick.

You know what Alex? He never said a word, never asked me about it, never offered advice, nothing. He was just there. Coming over and mowing the lawn, shoveling snow or just hanging out with me and Jake. Do you know it was Josh who taught Jake to ride a bike and to catch a baseball? So if I'm here and Josh is here, who's taking care of Jake?" she finished in a whisper.

Alex didn't know what to say. All these years Dara had been dealing with this on her own. She felt very small and shallow. She and Emily had just given up on her and Josh hadn't. Josh's outburst the night before came back to her. She had thought he was just blowing off steam but telling Dara he would kill someone to protect her made more sense now. How self-involved and selfish can a person be? Alex was forced to admit she had been oblivious to Dara's pain for years.

"Dara, I'm so sorry. I was a terrible friend to just let you go like that. I'm sorry I didn't fight for our friendship." she said with shame.

"Oh Alex, don't. I'm just as much to blame. I pushed you guys away instead of telling you what was happening. We were just kids and I didn't know what to do. It seemed easier to just hide from everyone." Dara reached out and took Alex's hand.

"What about your Dad? Did he know? Did you tell him?" Alex asked.

With a bitter laugh and shake of her head Dara told her, "He knows. At first, he took us more often but he got remarried and was busy with his new wife. We still went every other weekend and he would do Dad stuff with us, like movies and camping. I loved when he would take us to the firing range. He would introduce us to his work friends and they would all gather around to watch me shoot. It was such a great feeling, an escape from dealing with my Mom. Then his new wife, Sandy had twins and he stopped doing those things with us. Jack was still little so he thought it was neat to have two babies around but as soon as they were over a year old, I was nothing but a babysitter for my Dad. The last weekend I spent with them was over a year ago and when we got to their house Friday night, Dad and my step-mom left for a night out within minutes. The next day they went out shopping and then they brought us home pizza and movies and left for another night out. Sunday morning my Dad woke me up and asked me to feed the twins breakfast and when I got mad and told him I felt like I was only there for free babysitting, he said he'd give me some money. After that I wouldn't go to his place anymore. He would still take Jack but he started bringing him home earlier and earlier and then he would miss a weekend until he just stopped coming at all." She paused to take a shaky breath and finished with "I don't have a Dad."

Alex didn't know what to say. She had no idea what Dara's life had become and was at a loss for words. Dara scrubbed her face with her hands and let out an angry breath. "I should have never come on this trip. I had it all set up so that Jake would be having sleepovers at a couple different friends' houses. He wouldn't have to stay at home with our Mom. With all of this happening, no one is going to be having sleepovers. He's only eight and he's all alone. I'm so selfish. I just wanted one thing for me. One thing that was happy and I could be, be…" Dara trailed off.

"A kid." Alex finished for her.

"Yeah, a kid, not taking care of Jake, cleaning up my Mom or being mad at my Dad. Just free for a few days. Free to be a kid, and now because of that selfish decision, my little brother is all alone and in danger." she said angrily.

"Jake's fine." came from the doorway. Both girls looked up startled to see Josh standing there. "He's with my Dad."

"What are you talking about, why would he be with your Dad?" Dara asked, confused.

Josh entered the room and sat down beside Dara, taking her hand. "Before I left, I told my Dad everything about your situation. I asked him to keep an eye on Jake. I also told Jake that if anything happened he was to go to my Dad for help. As soon as the lights went out, my Dad would have gone and got him. Jake is safe Dara."

Dara stared at Josh with open mouthed astonishment until she could choke out "Jake's safe. Thank you, thank you." And she dissolved into tears of relief. As Josh took her into his arms, Alex slipped out of the room to give them some privacy.

** ** ** ** ** **

Alex came out of the house and headed towards the old camper to see what the boys were up to. She saw Quinn wrestling with a large propane tank and he set it by the back of the motorhome. Wiping sweat from his face, he saw Alex approaching and gave her a smile. "Hey, where are Josh and Dara? I thought we should have a meeting to plan things out. I sent Josh in to get you guys."

Stalling for them she told him "They're just in the middle of something. Why don't I throw some lunch together? We can eat while we talk. Oh, and before I forget, there's a gun safe in the basement. We need to look for keys for it." she said, hoping to distract him.

"That's great! Hopefully we won't need them but it's good to be prepared just in case. Let's have lunch on the patio and we'll look at the maps we found in the camper."

Alex went over to the bikes and pulled out the ham pancakes she had made this morning as well as the apples and carried them over to the patio table. She went inside the house and got some cans of soda and a pile of napkins. As she was heading back out she stopped at the door to the basement and called down the stairs, "Lunch is ready! Meeting on the patio in five minutes!" and continued out onto the patio.

Alex looked over at the fresh graves of the Petersons. The poor dog was still lying beside them and Alex was again saddened that she didn't even know its name. She went back in to the house and got a bowl and filled it with water from a jug. She took it out and placed it beside the dog, hoping it would show some interest. The dog looked up at her with the saddest eyes and gave a small whine then laid its head back down. Close to tears, Alex moved away and sat at the patio table waiting for the others. She was wondering if the dog would stay there until it died or if they should try to take it with them when Cooper and Quinn joined her.

Quinn followed Alex's gaze and with a sigh sat down beside her. "There's nothing we can do Alex. The dog will stay there and die or it'll go wild. We can't take it with us. We have enough on our plates without having to care for a dog. I'm sorry." he said, rubbing her arm.

"I know. It's just so sad. With all the death and destruction of the last few days, that one dog is so heartbreaking is silly. I can't help feeling so sad for it."

Cooper leaned toward her "It's not silly, Alex. Being able to be sad for one dog after all the death you've seen is a good thing. I think by the time we get home, we will all be hardened to a lot of things. So be sad when you can and take joy and happiness where you find them. Only when you stop feeling should you be worried. And right now what I'm feeling is……hungry!" he joked, lightening the mood.

Josh and Dara came out of the house and took seats at the table. Dara's eyes were red and puffy but she seemed composed. Everyone took a ham pancake and apple and started eating.

Josh finished his pancake quickly and said, "This is pretty good Alex, but now that we have a working stove and oven we can have better meals. The fridge works too so we can keep things longer. What do you guys think about taking a few laying hens with us for eggs? There are some fold up cages that would fit in the back of the truck. And if we have to, we can get rid of them for roasted chicken dinner. I also found a spring room under the barn. It has cheese and butter as well as some meat so even though the freezer part of the fridge is small, we can still take some of it."

Quinn was nodding, "That's a good idea Josh. A few hens and we can have fresh eggs that we can stock up on in the fridge. They would also be good for barter. So, I think we should stay here for the rest of the day and night and head out first thing in the morning. We need to stock the camper and truck up and hopefully find a way to fill up the water tanks on the camper. Alex found a gun safe in the basement, so we need to find keys for it and see what's in it. I also think we should go over these road maps we found and see if we can find a way to get around Las Vegas without getting too close to it. It's going to be nasty around that city. It would be good if we could map out a few different routes around all the major cities we need to get past. Travelling on back roads and secondary highways might be our best bet. The interstate is going to be packed with cars and people." He looked around the nodding group and finished with, "Ok, let's get packed up and sorted out. I say we have a BBQ for our supper and get a good night's rest and then head for home."

Chapter 10

Three days later and Alex was looking out at yet more barren scrub covered desert. They had taken a secondary highway at Baker that went north into Death Valley. The good news was that it would take them far from Las Vegas and there were no real towns on the highway. The bad news was there was nothing else either. Desert and rock, as far as the eye could see. There were hardly any cars on the road which meant that they could make good time, keeping at a steady forty miles an hour in case they came up on anything blocking the road. They were keeping the speed down, not wanting to risk losing one of the priceless vehicles to an accident. They had made around three hundred miles the day before and it had been uneventful except for one brief encounter.

They had gone north, skirting the Nellis Air Force Range Complex, which was nothing more than more scrub covered desert and rock, when they had seen a dust cloud moving towards them out of the desert. It could only be another vehicle raising a line of dust like that, so they pulled over and got into defensive positions.

They had talked about different scenarios and how they would handle them, so they all knew what to do. They all had guns, thanks to Mr. Peterson's gun safe but they kept them tucked away. Only Quinn and Cooper had shotguns on display and those were held pointed up. The idea was to warn off anyone looking for a fight, not start one.

Quinn and Cooper were standing with the truck bed between them and the approaching vehicle, ready to duck down for cover if shooting started. Alex, Dara and Josh were in the scrub bushes further back on their side of the road. They didn't want to be trapped in the camper if bullets started flying.

As the dust cloud got closer, they were able to make out an older model army looking jeep. It had two men with rifles in the front seat. It came to a stop by swerving sideways and both men jumped out on the far side, using it as cover.

"This is a United States Air Force patrol. Step into the road and identify yourselves!"

Quinn and Cooper whispered to each other and then Quinn shouted back, "How do we know you guys are really soldiers or are just trying to get the jump on us?"

"Sir, the only way I can confirm that is to show you my ID. If you would be willing to come forward unarmed, I would meet you halfway." the man yelled back.

After more whispered discussion between the boys, Quinn held his shot gun high in the air and set it down in the truck bed. Walking around the side of the truck, he kept his hands in the air and made his way to the side of the road closest to the jeep. He stopped halfway between the two vehicles and made sure he wasn't blocking Coopers' line of sight. The man who had been doing the yelling came around the jeep and walked towards Quinn. He was dressed in a camouflage outfit and had a gun in a holster at his side but had left his rifle in the jeep.

When he reached a few feet from Quinn his faced showed surprise, "You're just a kid!"

Quinn was used to that response by now and shrugged it off. "Are you guys really from the Army?" he asked.

"Air Force Son, there's a difference. What are you doing out here? And where did you get two working vehicles? Are your parents with you?" the soldier questioned.

"Sir, do you have any identification? We're trying to be careful with who we give answers to." Quinn evaded.

"What? Oh sure. Hold on."

The soldier pulled out a billfold and handed Quinn a card with his picture and information on it. Major Tom Lewis was the name on the ID card. Quinn handed it back and asked "Isn't a Major a little high up to be out on patrol, Sir?"

The Major smiled, "I'm not really on patrol, son. I just wanted to get away from the airport and see what there is to see. I didn't really expect to run into anyone out here. Now, can I ask again, who are you, what are you doing out here and are your parents over behind those trucks?"

"My name is Quinn and I'm with some friends. We were on a class trip when everything stopped working. We are trying to get home and thought it would be easier if we stayed off the main highways. We helped an elderly man bury his wife and he gave us his truck and camper to help us get home." He quickly summarized, "Do you know what happened Sir? Can you give me any information? We are headed north to Canada and anything you could tell us would be appreciated."

The soldier studied Quinn and seemed to reach a decision. "Do you know what an EMP is Quinn?" At his nod the soldier continued "It was set off somewhere above Kansas and it basically shut everything electrical down all over most of the continent. Northern Mexico and Southern Canada will have been affected. Europe was hit as well. I'm sure you've figured out, older mechanical things will still work but anything modern has been fried. Nothing touched down in North America but I can't say the same for the Mid East. Not much left there that's not glowing. We've got all our boys headed home but it'll take a while to get them back. We can expect aid from some countries but a lot are out of business. Until then, things are going to be real ugly in this country. Why are you going to Canada?"

It took a minute for Quinn to process all that the soldier had said and realise he had asked a question. "That's where we're from. We live in central Alberta." was his distracted answer.

"Central Alberta? That would be a good area to ride this out. Lots of farm land, cattle and not a lot of cities. Well you kids are lucky to have working trucks. Stay on the back roads as much as possible and watch out because those trucks will make you a big tempting target. I won't hold you up. Get going and good luck Quinn. I hope you make home." The Major said and he turned and walked back to his jeep.

Quinn slowly walked back to the trucks thinking of nuclear war and all it might mean in the future.

After he had shared the news with the rest of the group they got back on the road and travelled for a few more hours before stopping and setting up camp for the night. Sleeping in the camper was much more comfortable than sleeping on the ground and making meals on the stove was much faster and easier. Alex and Dara had stocked every spare inch of the camper with food supplies from Mr. Peterson's basement and kitchen. They had plenty of baking supplies so she had made use of the camper's small oven and baked buns so they would have bread.

Staring out the window Alex was happy they were almost into Utah. She hoped the landscape would change. She was so bored and it made her think of all the things that used to fill a long road trip that wouldn't work now. Portable DVD players to watch movies on, IPods for music, even a DS to play video games were all obsolete now. She wished she had a deck of cards. At least she could play solitaire on the camper's small dining room table.

Alex looked towards the front of the camper where Josh was driving and Dara was sitting in the passenger seat. Dara's hair looked great. Before leaving Mr. Peterson's house they had played beauty shop and colored out all the blue streaks. The dark chestnut color really made her grey eyes stand out. Having plenty of water from the pump on the well, they had all gotten to clean up and wash out their clothes properly. The tanks on the camper were filled with water but they were being very careful with how much they used so for now it was back to baby wipes and wash cloth baths. With a sigh, Alex turned back around in her seat and looked out the side window, "I'm soooo bored!" she thought to herself and was jumping in shock as a gun shot went off and the camper jerked towards the middle of the road.

"Hold on and get your guns ready!" Josh yelled at them as he brought the camper back into the right lane.

Alex was trying to see what was going on out the window when a pair of motorcycles came up beside them. Another two were on either side of the old truck that Quinn and Cooper were in ahead of them. All of the motorcycle riders were rough looking men in dirty jeans and leather jackets. They also all had sawed off shot guns and while one of the riders waved Josh over to stop, the other one pointed the gun at the front tire. Alex looked ahead and saw that Quinn and Cooper were being threatened the same way.

"What do we do Josh? Should I open the window and shoot at them?" Alex yelled.

"Damn it, no! It's too late; they got us covered from behind as well. Quinn's pulling over. FUCK! FUCK! Dara, get in the back. Hide the guns and find a knife and put it in your boot, Alex you too. Hurry, I have to pull over." Josh yelled, frantic.

Dara scrambled into the back with Alex and they both started to reach for the kitchen cutlery drawer at the same time, wrenching it all the way out and spilling utensils all over the floor. Dara's hiking boots were higher than Alex's so she grabbed a paring knife out of the mess and slid it down the side of her boot. Alex was franticly searching for the red handled Swiss army knife she knew was in the drawer before she finally found it under the table. She stuck it down the inside of her boot and quickly started to scoop up the utensils back into the drawer and slammed it back into the cupboard just as Josh came to an abrupt stop, sending her back down to the floor. Beside her head was a small door that gave access to the stove and oven mechanics and Alex quickly stuffed her gun in it as far back as possible. She scrambled back onto her feet and rushed to the front to see what was happening, almost crashing into Dara, who was frozen stiff behind Josh in the driver's seat.

"What's going on?" she asked with a note of hysteria in her voice.

~ 102 ~

"Don't move Alex. They have a gun pointed at Josh's head." Dara whispered.

Alex looked ahead and saw both Quinn and Cooper kneeling on the road behind the truck with two of the bikers covering them with shot guns. Just as she was about to say something, there was a banging on the side door of the camper that made her jump. Dara turned to her slowly and with a blank face and flat tone said, "Open the door Alex. We have no choice."

Alex's heart was pounding with the need to do something. Fight or flight and it took her a moment to realize that Dara was right. With all the boys covered, there was nothing to do but follow along and see what happens. She stepped back towards the side door and reached out to open the door. As soon as the latch clicked open, the door was ripped open and a stubby shot gun barrel was pointed up at her. The man holding it was rough looking with greasy hair and had tattoos covering both of his arms, all the way up the sides of his neck. He looked Alex up and down and with a sleazy sneer, motioned her out with the barrel of his gun.

"Hello princess. Come on out of there and join our little party." he looked past Alex and saw Dara. "You too, sweet cheeks. Nothing funny or your prom dates will be minus their heads." he told them with a hard look as he backed up to let them out.

Alex felt Dara put a hand on her shoulder and squeeze it before giving a small push to get her moving. As soon as they stepped down, another ugly man grabbed them by the arms and started to pull them towards the front of the camper. He was squeezing Alex's upper arm so hard she expected to have finger print bruises. As they came closer to the kneeling boys, he let go and gave them a big push, sending both the girls staggering towards Quinn and Cooper. Both the boys had blank faces but when Alex stumbled into Cooper, he reached out to steady her and received a shot gun stock to his ribs.

"Keep your hands up Romeo!" barked the biker who was watching him. "You don't have to worry about your girlfriend. We'll take real good care of her." he sneered. "On the ground girlies!" he waved them down.

Alex and Dara lowered themselves to their knees beside the two boys and put their hands up. Josh was pulled out of the camper and shoved their way as well. The man behind him was prodding him along with the barrel of the shot gun. As he was pushed into a stumble again, Josh growled and made to turn around and fight but before he could, one of the men grabbed him and shoved him down beside Dara with a, "Don't get brave boy," comment.

The kids were all lined up on their knees between the two vehicles with two of the armed men watching them and the other four searching through the camper and truck. They were all silent and Alex took a quick look at Quinn but he stared straight ahead with a grim face. The four men came together in front of the camper and had a conference. Alex couldn't hear what they were saying but they kept looking over at the line of kids and with a big laugh they stared their way.

The biggest biker of the bunch came forward and stood in front of them. He walked back and forth looking the kids over one by one. He was well over six feet tall with muscular arms and a barrel chest. His shaved head gleamed in the dessert sun and when he walked past, Alex saw that he had a skull tattoo covering the back of his head. He finally stopped his inspection and gave them an amused look.

"Well if it isn't the cast of High School fucking Musical. So nice of you all to bring these goodies into my territory." his wave took in the two vehicles full of supplies. "So what do you think I should do with you boys? The girls will be coming with us for a little recreation time but I don't really see a need for you three," he paused menacingly. "Then again, it does get boring now so we could use you boys for a little game I came up with to entertain the troops. Yup I think we can have some fun with these three. Where were you kids headed to?" he asked.

When no one answered him, his face darkened and he lifted a huge boot and planted it in Josh's stomach. Josh crumpled to the road with a groan and he lay in a fetal position, trying to get a breath. Dara made a small gasp when he had kicked Josh and that made him turn his attention towards her.

"Let's try that again. You look like you want to spare your boyfriend some hurt, so why don't you answer my question."

He reached down and seemed to tenderly tuck a lock of Dara's hair behind her ear. With a soft smile on his face he completed the move by grabbing a bunch of her hair and wrenched her head back, making her face up towards him. Tears sprang to her eyes and started flowing down her face. With a shaking voice she told him, "North. We were headed north into Utah!"

With her answer, he shoved her backwards making her fall on her butt. "That wasn't so hard now was it?" he beamed a smile at her. He looked to the rest of the kids and told them, "Listen up! My name is Skull and I run this outfit. When I ask a question, I get an answer! You lot are in for a world of hurt but it's up to you just how bad it gets." Skull turned to his men and ordered "Search them and get them loaded up into that camper. Let's get back to the base. I need a beer!" With that, he turned and walked over to a huge motorcycle and lit up a cigarette.

His men pulled each of the kids to their feet and patted them down. The girls were groped and Alex fought hard not to make a sound and give them the satisfaction they wanted. The men didn't find the knives that the girls had in their boots and Alex took a bit of hope away that they might get a chance to use them in the future. After they had been searched, all of their hands were zip tied behind their backs and they were roughly shoved and pushed back over and into the camper. The bikers made them all sit on the floor and it was extremely uncomfortable with their hands tied. The camper was driven by one of the men and another was sitting at the dinette keeping his gun trained on them. All Alex could see was the two barrel holes of the shot gun pointing at her face and she couldn't help but think that she would never complain again, because sometimes being bored is good.

Chapter 11

Quinn sat next to his Grandfather on the wide tractor seat. He kept his head down and eyes on the ground that moved past as they drove to the back fields. His Grandpa had insisted he come out to the fields with him today, even though all Quinn wanted to do was stay in the room they had given him and stare up at the ceiling. It's where he had spent every day since his parent's funeral.

He had just had his eighth birthday and his Dad and Mom had promised him a trip to the Calgary Stampede for his present. He was so excited to make the trip down to the city and could hardly wait the month and a half until they were going. He had been having a sleep over at a friend's house when his Grandpa had shown up and taken him home. It was really weird because his Grandparents lived an hour away and they didn't babysit him normally. When they had gotten home he was surprised that his parents weren't there waiting for him.

It was then that Grandpa had sat him down and explained about the car accident and that his Mom and Dad would not be coming home. He had run through the house, checking every room for them, unable to believe that they were gone. His Grandpa had finally caught up to him and tried to hold him but Quinn had hammered at him with his small fists and screamed that he was a liar. It wasn't until he saw the tears streaming down the older man's face, that the fight drained out of him and he collapsed.

After that, everything was a blur and Quinn felt like a zombie. He was frozen all through his extended family members gathering and through the funeral and burial. He didn't want to think or feel. All the things he would no longer have in his life with his parents gone was too much for him to process, so he locked it all deep inside and went through the motions and did what he was told.

After the funeral, his grandparents sat him down and explained that he would be coming to live with them and his home would have to be sold. It was that final thing that finally broke through his paralysis. Not only had he lost his family but now he was losing his home and moving away from everything he knew and it broke him. He didn't have many memories of what happened after that but it was a blur of screaming and crying. He remembered clearly looking over his Grandpa's shoulder, back at his home as he was carried away to the truck but that was all. It had been five days since then and Quinn had not spoken a word since.

"I love this view. There's nothing more satisfying than looking out over my plowed and planted fields, knowing that I'm providing for my family with my own hard work. One day this will all be yours Quinn. I hope you will come to love it as well." his Grandpa told him.

Quinn looked up from the passing field and scanned ahead. The plowed field ran ahead in rows that looked like they had fuzzy green moss growing on them and Quinn realized that it was the crop just starting to grow. Further in the distance the field ended at a forest that went as far as he could see. White topped mountains rose against the horizon. It was pretty and the air smelled sweet with the scent of freshly turned earth. Looking out in the distance, Quinn felt the beginnings of a peace settle into him.

"You know, your father used to run through these fields like a banshee. He was always up to some project or adventure. He went camping by himself back in those trees and would have his friends over for all kinds of games. You could be happy here, Quinn. I know it doesn't feel like you will ever be happy now but in time you will. Your Mom and Dad wanted everything for you. They would want you to enjoy life and not grieve forever. I know your Dad would be happy to see you running the same fields he did. Just give it a chance, son."

Quinn felt tears fill his eyes and quickly blinked them away. He thought about his Dad camping in the woods as a boy and wished they could do it together. He was lost in thought when his Grandpa said "Now who do we have here?"

Quinn's head came up and he saw four kids standing at the fence line waiting for them. There were three girls and one stocky boy. As they got closer one of the girls yelled out a greeting. She had red gold hair that gleamed in the sun. "Hey Mr. D. Who you got with you there?"

Quinn's Grandpa stopped the tractor beside the group and shut it down so they didn't have to yell. "Hey yourself, Alex. This here is my grandson, Quinn. He's come to live with us. What are you kids up to today?" he smiled down at her fondly.

The kids all studied Quinn with interest and curiosity. It wasn't often that a new potential playmate moved into their area. They all knew what had happened to Quinn's parents and the meet was a set up by the adults to try to draw Quinn out.

It was Alex who answered him. "We're headed back into the forest to build a club house. We got hammers and nails and a hatchet. It's going to be our home base for the summer." She looked to Quinn again and then to her friends. "Hey Quinn, do you want to come with us? We could really use someone else to help us build."

Quinn felt a surge of excitement. Go into the forest and build a club house? With no adults? How cool. He was about to jump down when he remembered his parents and his shoulders sagged. How could he go off on an adventure when his parents were dead? He looked down at his feet and stayed silent.

"Dude, I'm seriously outnumbered here and if you don't come, these girls are going to totally boss me around. Help a brother out?" the stocky boy pleaded.

"Yeah right Josh! We're the ones that will end up doing most of the work while you mess around. Seriously Quinn, our friend David is away and we need at least one boy who can pull his weight." said the brown haired girl, with piercing grey eyes.

"Just give it a chance Quinn." his grandfather said quietly, so only he could hear.

Quinn looked into his Grandpa's eyes and saw such love and hope in them. He felt his heart lift. He turned and looked down at the kids waiting for his answer and slowly nodded his head. The boy named Josh gave a whoop and did a funky little dance on the spot and the girls all smiled up at him.

Alex waved him down off the tractor. "Let's go! We brought a lunch so we'll feed him Mr. D. and we'll have him back by supper. Come on guys. We've got a lot to do!" and she turned and headed towards the tree line.

Quinn climbed down the tractor and ducked through the fence. The three girls had already made it almost to the trees but the boy, Josh, had stayed waiting for him.

"Alright Dude! You really saved my bacon. They still have us outnumbered but at least now I've got some back up." As the two boys followed the girls into the woods Josh leaned over and stage whispered "What do you know about cherry bombs?"

That summer, Quinn's new friends slowly pulled him back to life. They filled a part of the void that his parents had left in his heart. He slowly built a new family with his grandparents and friends and he did everything he could to help them and keep them safe.

** ** ** ** ** ** ** ** ** **

The motor home swerved to avoid a car wreck, throwing Quinn into Cooper and bringing him out of his memories. The kids were crammed into the small amount of floor space in the camper. The biker guarding them was named Snake. He had a tattoo of a snake that coiled around his neck. His greasy hair and dirty clothes reeked of body odor and stale cigarette smoke. He had been keeping up a running commentary on all the nasty things that he planned to do to the girls.

Quinn looked over to Dara and Alex and was relieved to see that they both seemed to be unaffected by the man's rant. Alex seemed to be far away in thought with a blank expression on her face. Dara had a look of concentration and was focused down at her feet. Josh had his back to her and she seemed to be nudging his bound hands with her boot. Josh kept trying to grasp her foot but with his hands tied he was having trouble getting a good grip. Quinn didn't know what the two were trying to do but he didn't want to bring attention to them so he looked away.

They were sitting on the floor and there was no way to see out the window to where they were going but based on the movements of the camper they hadn't left the highway they had originally been traveling on. At least they were going in the right direction, Quinn thought.

A sharp intake of breath from Dara made him look back to her and Josh. Quinn saw her sock start to turn red with blood and was confused until he saw the knife clutched between Josh's bound hands. Quinn realized that Dara must have had a knife in her boot and Josh had managed to free it. Josh held the knife until the next time the camper swerved and used the motion to arch forward and slide it down the back of his pants. He then slowly pulled his shirt out of his pants and let it hang down to cover the back of his pants. When he was done he slowly wiggled and shifted until he was sitting sideways and could meet Quinn's eyes. Quinn gave him a brief nod of understanding just as a boot was shoved against Josh's side.

"What's a matter, big boy? You gotta go potty?" Snake taunted him in baby talk. When he got no response from Josh, he chuckled and said "Don't worry. You'll be pissin' your pants soon enough." and he let out a laugh that sounded like a donkey braying.

The driver didn't turn around but yelled back "Shut the hell up Snake! Leave them kids be until we get back to base. We don't need any problems or Skull will be using us for entertainment tonight."

"Ah shit, I'm just havin' a little fun." he mumbled like a chastised child.

After that, there wasn't any more talking and it seemed to Quinn that they had been driving for about an hour when the camper began to slow down. They all swayed to one side as the camper made a turn and they could feel the road change to a rougher surface. It was only five minutes when they made another turn and came to a stop. The driver came around his seat and pointed a hand gun at them.

"All right kiddies, everybody off the bus." and motioned them up. It was difficult to stand with their hands tied and finally Snake reached down and started to haul them to their feet. The driver opened the side door and bright sunshine filled the inside of the camper. He climbed down and motioned them to get out.

It was a relief to be outside in the fresh air. The smell of nasty sweat from the two bikers was enough to make them gag. Quinn took a look around and saw that they were parked in a graveled area that had ten motorcycles and a large white panel van. The building was a long one story structure; an old store with a living area attached. There was an old style set of gas pumps on the far end that looked like they hadn't been used in decades. A rough shove sent Quinn forward and he followed his friends toward the building. He looked at his friends and vowed that whatever happened he would do whatever it took to free them.

As Alex walked through the door, it took a few minutes for her eyes to adjust from the sun's brightness to the dim interior. She tried to avoid the trash that was strewn around on the floor, but the place was a mess with empty beer cans and glass liquor bottles and other junk. As the room came into focus she could make out a couple of old leather couches and a glass coffee table overflowing with filled ashtrays, beer cans and dirty glasses. There were two dirty women with stringy, greasy hair wearing skin tight jeans and low cut tight shirts sprawled on the couches. The women looked over with glassy eyes and not much interest when the kids were pushed into the room. Alex was shoved to the side when the leader, Skull, entered and barely kept her balance when one of the other bikers pushed her back the other way. Skull strode over to the two women and grabbed one of them and hauled her to her feet.

"Get up you lazy cow! Can't you see we have guests? Go get the ropes so we can hook them up!" he yelled as he turned the woman and booted her in the butt, propelling her towards a door in the back of the room. He flopped down into the spot the woman had just occupied and started to search through the piles of empty beer cans. When he didn't find what he was looking for, his face turned even harsher and he let out another bellow.

"DOG!!! Get in here!"

Within seconds, a short, skinny weasel faced man rushed into the room. In his hand was a dog leash and attached to it on all fours was a small boy of about eight or nine. He was naked except for a pair of dirty underwear that had rocket ships on them. His skinny body was covered with bruises and scrapes and what looked like burns. When he lifted his head up, Alex could see he had a black eye and crusted blood under his nose. With all the damage done to the child, it was the utter emptiness behind his eyes that broke Alex's heart.

"Rat, let Dog of his leash. I want a beer… Make it two!" Snake commanded.

"Sure boss, sure." Rat said in a rush and reached down to unhook the leash from the collar around the child's neck. "You heard him Dog! Go get some beer and make it quick." He punctuated the order with a boot to the child's bottom. The boy made no sound as he scrambled back out of the room.

Skull turned towards the other woman still lounging on the other couch. "We're having a party tonight Baby. We've got some entertainment and I want a good meal. Go on out to that camper we just brought in. I took a quick look and they have it stocked up with all kinds of food. Get some stuff and you and Sheila can make us a feast."

The woman stretched lazily and came to her feet. She sauntered over and straddled Skull. "If I make you a good meal, do you promise to share the entertainment with me later?" she asked him seductively.

Skull leaned back on the couch and looked the woman up and down with a smile. Suddenly he bucked his hips and the woman flew backwards, landing on the floor between the coffee table and couch. Her head banged against the table, sending empty beer cans and ashtrays flying. She scrambled to her feet rubbing her head.

"Damn it, Skull! Why'd you do that for?" she whined.

"Take a good look Baby." he motioned to Dara and Alex. "Fresh meat, you watch yourself or one of them will be your permanent replacement." He then bellowed out a huge laugh at the look on the woman's face. "Get cookin' Baby! And make it good. I'm tired of the crap you two have been feeding us."

With a look of hatred directed at Alex and Dara she stormed out to raid the camper.

The other woman Sheila, came back into the room with her hands full of rope. Her voice was whiney when she handed the pile to one of the bikers. "We only have four sets of hooks put up so one of them won't be hung up."

"Whatever! Popper, just tie one of those boys to a chair for now. He can replace whoever dies first. Sheila, go out and help Baby in the camper. Popper, you and Rat get them kids secured in the back room. DOG!!! Where's my damn beer." he roared suddenly. The child came running into the room with two beer cans clutched to his chest. He placed them on the table in front of Skull and quickly dodged a back hand headed his way. The boy retreated into the farthest corner of the room and curled himself up.

Alex felt a man come up behind her and her bound wrists were pulled up higher that her arms would bend. She leaned forward to ease the pressure and felt the man push himself against her bottom. "Yeah baby, that's the ticket" he breathed into her ear." Alex shuddered in disgust but said nothing. There was no point in antagonizing these men. It would be better to comply and wait for her chance to do something.

The pressure on her arms went away suddenly and Alex realized that the plastic zip tie had been cut. She quickly brought her hands in front of her and tried to rub the circulation back into them. Looking at her friends she saw that they had all been freed but they were having each wrist tied individually, with a loop left over. It didn't make sense to Alex, until she remembered what the woman said about hooks. Her shoulders tensed at the thought of hanging by her arms from hooks. As they were shoved into the back room, Alex craned her neck around to get one more look at the child curled up in the corner. Instead of being afraid, she felt a huge rage settle over her and sent a silent promise to the child that she would free him and give him vengeance.

Chapter 12

The room Alex was shoved into was sparsely furnished. It had an old ragged futon against one wall and a folding table against another. There was another door leading to a different room on the third wall. The main feature of the room was two pairs of thick metal hooks anchored to the fourth wall just above head height. Under the hooks, the wall was scuffed and had grooves in it that looked like heel indentations. There were also many dark brown stains that looked like rust but Alex guessed that they were dried blood stains.

The hooks had obviously been used before and Alex gave a shudder at the fate of the previous occupants. When Dara saw the hooks she started to struggle with the biker that had her arm in his grip. Alex was surprised and proud of her friends for staying calm so far. The biker named Popper back handed Dara across the face and she fell to the floor clutching her cheek. The other man, Rat, pulled a gun from the matching pair strapped to his thighs.

"I've got them covered. Go ahead and get the girls on the wall." he told Popper.

Popper hooked a foot under a small step stool that was under the table and sent it sliding across the floor towards the wall with the hooks. He reached down and hauled Dara to her feet and dragged her over to the wall. Still stunned from the blow to her face, Dara didn't struggle. He positioned the stool between the hooks and shoved Dara up on it and turned her around so her back was against the wall. He raised her one arm and slipped the looped part of the rope over the hook and repeated it with her other arm. Once he had her positioned, he stepped back and once again hooked his foot under the step stool and yanked it out from under Dara's feet. She screeched in pain as her body dropped and her shoulder joints were stretched to hold her body weight. She could just barely reach the floor with her tippy toes. She snarled at the man as he patted her cheek.

"There you go princess. Get nice and comfy and I'll be back for you later." he said with a laugh.

He shoved the stool over between the next set of hooks and motioned Alex over. "Your turn Red."

Alex had been studying the ropes that Dara was hung up with and she knew how to save herself the shoulder pain. She climbed the stool and turned around before Popper had time to man handle her. When he hooked the first loop over the hook, she quickly twisted her wrist to get a grip on the rope and did the same with her other hand. She had practiced on the rings and bars for hours in gymnastics and knew she could hold her body weight with her arms positioned properly. Popper stepped back and eyed her up and down.

"You won't be so calm once the fun starts later." he taunted and kicked the stool out from under her feet. Alex was ready for it and tensed her arms. She let out a sound of pain so he wouldn't know she had control and he gave an evil chuckle.

"That's a small taste of what's to come baby girl."

The boys had stayed silent while Alex and Dara were strung up but as they were herded out of the room Quinn looked back at them.

"Stay strong. We'll find a way out of this."

He received a hard shove out of the room for his words, and then the door closed leaving the girls alone.

Alex slowly eased the tension in her arms, lowering herself to the floor and taking her weight onto her toes. She kept her wrists turned and her grip on the ropes so she could raise herself again if she needed to. Alex looked over at Dara and saw her friend had her head sagged forward.

"Are you okay, Dara?" she asked in concern. Dara slowly lifted her head and Alex wasn't surprised to see instead of defeat, rage blazed from her eyes.

"I'm going to kill all of these mother fuckers." Dara said through gritted teeth.

The girls heard banging, crashing and curses from the next room and painful moans. One of the boys was taking a beating and Alex thought it sounded like Josh.

"Ok bendy girl. Is there anything you can do to get us out of this? I saw what you did with the ropes. It has to be soon before they start in on us. My arms are already on fire." Dara said.

Before Alex could answer, loud heavy metal music came blaring from the other room. The girls looked at each other in confusion. How did these guys get a working stereo? Shaking her head, Alex tried to think of any way to get out of the ropes.

"There's nothing I can do like this." she told Dara, having to raise her voice over the music. "Without some kind of leverage…" she trailed off as the short biker named Rat came into the room.

He was as dirty and greasy as his friends. When he was bringing them into the room, Alex was surprised that she was taller than the man. He walked up between them and looked them over.

"Popper's busy havin' fun with your boyfriends and Skull sent the other guys out to town to bring back some friends of ours to join the party tonight, so I thought I'd come in and keep you from getting lonely. Maybe get myself a little taste of what's to come later." he told them with a leer.

Alex had been wracking her brain to think of some way to get out of the ropes and as she looked over at the disgusting man, it came to her in a flash. She just needed him to come over in front of her. She tensed her arms and raised herself up as if she was on the rings and taunted him.

"So what exactly do you think you're going to do with us, little man?" she asked him with as much contempt in her voice as she could muster.

His face flushed with anger at the "little man" comment and he rushed at her. As soon as he was in front of her but still a few steps away, Alex tensed her whole body and split her legs bringing them up on either side of him and then clamped them tightly on either side of his head so her body was jack knifed. Her shoulder joints and wrists were screaming in pain at the strain. The back of her knees were resting on the short man's shoulders and Alex kept her legs board straight and used the leverage and her strong stomach muscles to lift her upper body straight up. As soon as she came level with the hooks she lifted her arms, the loops of rope clearing the hooks. She then brought her arms across her chest and did a half twist sideways. Her arms shot out downwards so she would land on her hands but with her legs still clamped around the man's neck, he came with her to the side and they ended up in a heap on the floor.

The whole maneuver had only taken seconds. Alex found herself giggling and couldn't help thinking, "What a crappy dismount."

She shoved the man off her and jumped to her feet.

"Holy Crap, Dara! Did you see that? I can't believe that worked. I mean, that never should have worked out side of a movie!" she exclaimed in disbelief.

"Yeah yeah, you're a freakin' bendy super hero. Don't you think you should get his guns before he wakes up?" Dara joked.

The disbelief cleared from Alex's face as she dropped back down to the man. She rolled him over and had one gun out of its holster and was reaching for the other when she looked at his face. He was staring at her with a shocked look on his face. Alex fell back in surprise and pointed the gun at him. It only took a second to realize that he wasn't staring at her at all. There was no life behind the man's stare. He was dead. His head was canted to one side and Alex knew his neck was broken. The gun sagged in her grip and she let out a soft "Oh."

"Dara, I think he's dead. I killed him. I broke his neck." She said in a shocked whisper, staring at the dead man.

"Alex. Alex, look at me." she said sharply. When Alex looked up and met her eyes, she continued in a softer tone. "My arms really hurt Alex. Can you help me get down, please?"

Alex kept her eyes on Dara as she rose, not wanting to see the dead mans' shocked expression. In a trance, she went to the table and got the step stool and brought it over to Dara to stand on. As soon as she was free she went over to the body and pulled the other gun out of its holster. She then used her boot to flip him over so he was face down. She turned to Alex and put a hand on her shoulder. She could feel Alex shaking and she knew she had to get her back in the game if they were going to get out of this.

"Alex, I want you to really listen to me. Are you listening?" she gave her a little shake. When some of the shock had left Alex's eyes and she was focused Dara continued "That man was going to rape and torture us before he killed us in the most painful way. He put a dog collar on a child and beat him. That man was a monster. You killed him and that makes you a hero. Do you understand? By killing him, you saved me. You helped save all of us. You did the right thing and now I need you to put it aside because we need to go in there and save the boys and I'm going to need you for that. Are you with me?"

Alex took a deep breath and looked down at the gun in her hand. She pulled the slide back and chambered a round. "I'm with you." she said with stronger voice and a firm nod of her head.

Dara smiled "Alright! So Rat said that Skull sent the others into some town. I counted nine to start with, so with Popper next door, Skull and the two women that means we only have four more to deal with before the others get back. The music is going to help but I need…" She scanned the room and found what she was looking for on the futon. Dara went over and grabbed a throw pillow and brought it back. "Ok, we're going through that door and I'm going to shoot Popper right away. I'll shoot through the pillow to muffle the bang. Between that and the music no one should hear it. You be ready to shoot anyone else in the room. We get the boys free and then we go out to the main room and, well, we'll play that by ear. Boys free first, Ok?"

Just as Alex was going to answer, the song that was playing came to an end. They clearly heard Popper in the next room taunting one of the boys. As soon as the next song started Alex put her hand on the door knob and looked to Dara. Dara put the pillow over the end of the gun, took a deep breath and then nodded. Alex turned the knob and shoved. She stayed to the side so Dara could go through and as soon as she had past, followed her into the room with the gun raised, ready for anyone else that might be in the room. There was a muffled bang and then Popper crumpled to the floor. Once he was down, Alex had a clear view of Josh who was tied to a chair. His face was a mess of swelling and blood. Just as she was going to rush to him, he came free of the chair with a bloody knife in his hands.

"Damnit! If I knew you guys were going to rescue us, I wouldn't have cut the hell out of my wrists getting free." he said through mushy lips and collapsed back into the chair. Alex grabbed a wooden crate and slid it under Quinn's feet. As soon as he was getting free she rushed back to Josh. Grabbing his wrists, she turned them over to check the damage. They were bloody but none of the cuts were very deep. Alex whipped her sweat shirt off and then took her tank top off. She put her sweat shirt back on and reached down into her boots for the Swiss army knife she had put in there earlier. She cut up her tank top and used the strips to bind up Josh's wrists. She looked up to check his face injuries and saw that he was wide eyed.

"What?" she asked him in confusion.

"I just saw your boobs!" he said and grinned, causing him to wince from his split lips.

Alex couldn't help but laugh. Captured by bikers, tied up and beaten bloody and Josh was still Josh. She leaned over and kissed him on the cheek. "Well, consider it your reward for almost beating us girls to the rescue." she teased.

He leaned past her and looked to Popper, who was on the floor in a heap. "Is he dead?" Josh asked. Quinn had helped Cooper down and he went over and gave a hard kick to the man's ribs. When the man flopped over and made no sound, Cooper took a closer look.

"Yup, she shot him straight through the heart." He turned to Dara who had cracked the door and was peeking out into the main room. She eased the door closed and turned to the group.

Josh gave a wave and told her, "Nice shooting Tex!"

She gave him a quick grin and turned serious. She looked everyone over and in a determined voice said, "Ok guys, I'm ready to get out of here. Skull and his girlfriend are in there on the couch but I don't see the other woman. The rest of the gang was sent to town to bring friends for their party so we need to get going before they get back. Alex and I have hand guns and Cooper took the one off Popper. There's a sawed off shot gun over here in the corner you should grab Quinn. Josh, your eyes look kind of swollen so maybe stick with the knife for now. I say we just go right out with guns aimed and if they go for weapons we shoot them. Quinn, go to the left. That's where the boy went for beer so maybe the other woman is back there. Everyone agree?" she asked.

Everyone nodded and once Quinn had his weapon, they rushed out into the main room and spread out. Quinn went left and disappeared into another room. The rest all pointed their guns at the two on the couch. Skull sprang to his feet and the woman was quick to follow. He stood there glaring at the three guns pointing at them. Talk was impossible with the loud pumping music so Josh walked over and shut the stereo off. The silence was intense after the loud music and everyone paused for a moment. Alex saw the abused boy make his way closer to see what was happening.

Skull looked the group over and laughed "I can't believe the brat pack got the drop on my guys. What did you do, tie them up back there?" he scoffed.

"They're both dead and so will you be if you give us any trouble." Dara informed him in a cold voice.

"Yeah right! You kids don't have it in you to kill anyone. Put those guns down before I slap you silly." he threatened.

Skull caught movement out of the corner of his eye and saw the child inching closer to the kids. He lashed out with his foot, sending the boy flying and thundered "Get back in your corner Dog!"

Alex had time to think "You shouldn't have done that." when there was a loud gun shot and Skull flew back and crashed down through the glass coffee table, his chest pumping blood. The woman started screeching and went to her knees, trying to pull him back up. When she realized he was dead, she stood with a furious face and turned on Alex.

"I'm going to mess you up for that bitch." she screamed, spit flying out of her mouth.

Alex didn't know why the woman was yelling at her. She lunged toward Alex and another gunshot sounded, sending the woman to the floor.

"Wow Dara's on a rampage." she thought, turning to look at her friend.

Dara was looking back at her with surprise on her face. Alex looked to Cooper and Josh. They were all looking at her with surprise. She looked down at the gun in her hand and started to shake. She had shot them. She had killed another two people without even trying. Alex sank to her knees and started to sob.

Cooper came up and gently took the gun from her hand. He rubbed her back and tried to console her "It's Ok Alex. You did the right thing. You did good."

Alex barely heard him. She was so overcome with everything that happened today she felt lost. It was a small hand that crept into her own that brought her back to herself. She looked into the child's eyes and he croaked out a hoarse "Thank you." She remembered the silent vow she had made to him earlier and she had to smile at him because his eyes were no longer empty but filled with hope.

Chapter 13

When the shooting had started in the main room, Quinn had been in the kitchen. He had found the biker woman, Sheila making a meal out of food taken from the camper. With the shot gun pointed at her the woman was a crying, whining mess. She had tried to bargain with Quinn to let her go by offering all kinds of lewd activities. Quinn was disgusted with the woman and he ordered her to shut up. There was a roll of duct tape on the counter so he used it to bind her arms behind her back and had ripped a piece off to cover her mouth when she started to babble about kids and how it wasn't her fault and they couldn't blame her.

He stepped back and asked her "What kids? What are you talking about?"

She smiled at him, which only made her look more grotesque with her smeared make up and snot hanging from her nose. "If I tell you, will you let me go?" she whined.

Quinn brought the shot gun up and placed it against her forehead. In a cold voice he offered, "Or you could tell me and I won't kill you."

The woman squeaked and tried to scoot back away from the barrel of the gun. "OK, OK! I'll tell you! You don't have to get nasty. They found a bunch of kids on the highway a few days back. They were stranded in their school bus. Skull brought them back here. He was going to ransom them back to the town for supplies. That's where Dog came from. He's the sheriff's son and he mouthed off a lot so Skull was having some fun with him." She let out a giggle at the boy's torment that made Quinn want to vomit.

"Where are they?" he asked menacingly.

Once she told him where the kids were he turned the gun around and hit her in the head with the stock, knocking her out. Quinn had never hit a woman in his life and was raised to always respect and protect them but he made an exception for this one. She wasn't a woman to him but an animal.

Back in the main room, the others had spread out to check all the other areas and make sure they were alone. The boy hadn't left Alex's side and clung to her hand. He had told her his name was Luke but that was all Alex could coax out of him. Cooper had taken his shirt off and handed it to Alex, who put it on the boy to cover his damaged body. He seemed to snuggle into it and curled up against her. Everyone came back into the room reporting that the place was empty.

Just then Quinn came back in. His face was pale and his hands shook. He took in the two bodies on the floor with satisfaction and then looked to his friends.

"I need some help guys. We need to grab as much water as possible and come out to behind the house. Can someone go out front and keep watch? We don't want to be taken by surprise if the rest of the gang comes back." Quinn waved them to follow him.

Cooper went out front to keep watch and check on the camper and truck. The rest followed Quinn back through the kitchen. They all stepped over the unconscious woman and stopped to grab water bottles from the stack of cases piled in the corner. Quinn told them what Sheila had said to him about the kids and that he had gone out to the shed where they were being kept.

"When I opened that door, the wave of heat and the stench that rolled out almost knocked me off my feet. I thought they were all dead but the fresh air must have revived them because they started to move and groan. I pulled them all out into the shade. They need water badly." he finished and raced out the back door, arms filled with water bottles.

When Alex saw the eight kids leaning against the shed in the shade, she felt the tears start to roll down her face. She couldn't understand how anyone could do these horrible things to children. The sadness she felt at killing the three bikers left her and her heart hardened on the spot. She wished she had killed them all.

They were careful to only let the kids have small sips of water between wiping them down with the cool water. They carried them one by one into the house. Josh dragged the two bodies out of the main room and they placed the kids on the couches. Dara found a box of granola bars in the kitchen and once the children started to perk up she passed them out with orders to eat slowly or they would get sick. Other than being dehydrated and overheated, none of the kids seemed to have been abused. Luke had taken the punishment for being the Sheriff's son and for his feisty attitude. Alex left Luke in charge of monitoring his friends water intake and spread out with the others.

They took all the supplies they could find and piled them by the front door. Cooper had been told of the children and he was checking the white van out to see if it would run. They didn't have room in the truck and camper to take everyone with all the supplies. The van turned out to work and had been used by the bikers to bring the children here from their school bus. Cooper backed it up to the front door and they started to quickly load the loot as fast as they could. They knew the rest of the gang could return at any time. As they finished loading and were getting the kids moving, Josh came running in.

"You guys aren't going to believe what I just found in the basement!" he said excitedly.

They all rushed after him except for Dara who stayed to help the kids into the van. She had gathered all the pillows and blankets from the house and used them to pad the hard metal floor they would be traveling on. After their ordeal, she wanted to try and make them as comfortable as possible.

Luke had told them what town they were from and after checking the map, found it was on the highway they had been traveling on before the bikers stopped them. It was an hour's drive to get there so Dara put in water and easy to eat food for the children. It had been decided that Dara would drive the truck, Alex the camper and Josh the van. Quinn would ride in the back of the truck, armed and ready if they encountered any of the bike gang. Cooper had ripped the vent from the top of the camper and was to be another armed look out.

They would not be taken again.

The sight that greeted, Alex, Quinn and Cooper in the basement, brought them to a standstill. Two of the walls were covered in racks that were filled with what looked like assault rifles and cases of ammunition. The bikers had all been carrying sawed off shot guns or hand guns, so this many rifles was a shock. The other two walls and a few tables in the middle of the room had all kinds of drugs. There were bags filled with the white powder of cocaine, plastic tubs brimming with different coloured pills and tablets, huge bags full of marijuana and other things that they didn't recognize. After a few minutes of shocked silence while they took in the contents of the room. Quinn sprang into action.

"Grab as many guns as you can. Stack them in your arms and get them upstairs. Josh, grab that hand cart and let's load up all the ammo cases we can. We do two trips and then we need to get out of here." he said as he rushed forward and started to pile guns into Cooper's arms.

"What do we do about all that stuff?" Alex asked, waving at the drugs.

Without looking at her, Quinn replied in a cold determined voice "We burn it. We burn the whole place down."

When they brought out the first load, Dara had the children settled in the back of the van with the door still open. She did a double take when Alex walked past her with an armful of guns.

"Head in and help the guys while I get this stuff loaded up. I'll keep watch on the kids and the road." Alex told her over her shoulder.

They had already packed up the rest of the supplies so it was cramped in all the vehicles. Alex had to shove the guns anywhere she could fit them. The ammo boxes had to go into the van so they covered them with the blankets and pillows for the kids to sit on. After the second load was brought out and packed away, Quinn took two of the gas cans and went back inside. Everyone else loaded into their vehicles and got ready. Before Dara closed the van's back door she explained to the kids that it would be dark and get hot in there but it would only be for a little while and then they would be home. She told them they could bang on the wall connecting to the driver's compartment if they needed too and they would stop. The children were either still in shock or very brave because they all just nodded before she rolled the door down.

Quinn came through the door backwards, leaving a trail of gas. He threw the empty gas can back through the door and turned to check if everyone was ready. He caught site of the motorcycles. One of his friends had trashed them all. They were nothing more than a pile of chrome and rubber, never to be ridden again. He laughed with pleasure and turned to his waiting friends.

"Alex, Josh, you guys move out to the road and wait. I'm going to light this up and then Dara and I will take the lead. Josh, keep the van and the kids in the middle. Cooper, be ready. If you see a motorcycle just open fire, don't wait. We will get these kids home." he declared and waved them out.

He pulled a road flare out of his back pocket, lit it and threw it through the open door. He ran over and hopped into the back of the truck and grabbed a shot gun he had placed there. As soon as Dara saw that he was settled she pulled out to the road and got in front of the van. They had only gone half a mile when something in the house exploded and they could clearly see a black column of smoke rising. Dara watched the smoke in her side mirror and had a disturbing thought. She had opened the back sliding window before they left so she could talk to Quinn and she yelled his name through it to get his attention.

When he came close enough to hear she asked him, "What about that woman, Sheila? Was she still in there?"

Quinn shook his head. "I threw her into the shed where the kids were with a couple of bottles of water and a knife to cut herself free." he answered with indifference and turned back to scanning the road.

Dara gave a sigh of relief. There was a difference between defending themselves and others and flat out murder. She shook her head. She should have known that Quinn wouldn't have crossed that line.

She watched the road ahead with apprehension. After looking at the maps they had seen that the only town close to the gang's base was the one they were headed to so they guessed that it was the town the rest of the bikers had gone to. They had decided that they had a two and a half hour window before the gang made it back and found the destruction they had left. After discussing what to do if they met them on the road, they had all agreed that with the children riding with them and at risk in a shootout, it would be better to try and avoid them.

After about fifteen miles, Dara turned down a dusty gravel road and continued on it for a mile. She then did a U-turn to face back the way they had come and shut the engine off. The van and camper had a harder time turning around but after some back and forth they finally got lined up behind the smaller truck. They all got out and Dara rushed to open the rolling door on the van to give the children fresh air. She explained what they were doing and told them to sit tight, stay in the van so they could leave quickly and stay quiet so they could hear when the motorcycles went by. Once again, none of the kids answered her. They just sat blinking owlishly at her in the bright sunlight. Only Luke responded with a thumbs up.

Dara joined her friends at the front of the truck where Quinn was trying to figure out one of the assault rifles. After turning it over a few times, Cooper stepped forward and took it from his hands. He smoothly and competently ejected the magazine, turned it around and punched it back in. Next he pulled the cocking handle back. He then calmly handed it back to Quinn.

His friends were all staring at him in disbelief. "What? It's not a big deal. My old man always let me go with him to gun shows. They always had a shooting range set up and there was a gun dealer there that he knew. He always demonstrated different types of guns and let me hang out with him. I got pretty good with one of these. I can show you guys what to do if you want." he explained to them. They were still staring at him so he kept talking. "It might actually be a good idea. If these guys come after us, we don't want to be in a prolonged gun battle. These babies are really easy to use. You just point and spray. We could annihilate them in seconds. None of them were carrying these, just shot guns and hand guns. It would be no contest."

By the time he was done his face was bright red and he was beginning to wish he had kept his mouth shut. Cooper stared at his feet in misery as his friends looked to one another. It was Alex who stepped towards him and took his hand. He looked into her smiling sea green eyes and she said, "Show me."

Cooper had been showing them how to reload the guns and where the selector and safety was. He explained what the gun dealer had told him about shooting them. The gun barrel tended to rise as you shot it, so start aiming low and keep correcting down if you could. They all wanted to practice firing but knew that they had to stay quiet to hear the motorcycles going by. They had been on the side road for twenty five minutes when they heard the rumble of engines in the distance.

Dara ran to the back of the van and looked inside. Most of the kids were slumped down. Some were sleeping and others were sipping water or eating.

"Okay guys, we're going to be leaving in a minute. We are taking you all home and we're going to be going fast, so I want you all on the floor and try and brace yourselves in case we have to swerve around cars." Dara said with a smile as they started to scramble down onto the padded floor. She gave them a cheery wave and pulled the door down, flipping the latch so it wouldn't open while they were speeding down the road. She ran back to the truck and scanned ahead.

They couldn't see the highway from where they were parked but she could hear the engines very well. Dara had to remind herself to breath as she waited for the noise to fade in the distance. They waited a few more minutes to let the bikers get further down the road and then she jumped in the truck and they all started their vehicles up and slowly made their way back to the main highway. They turned right onto the paved road and quickly started to accelerate. They had to weigh the cost of safely getting around car crashes with the certainty of being chased once the gang discovered the ruins of their home. They all knew without a doubt that the bikers would come after them. It was whether or not they would make it to town first which was in doubt.

The three drivers went as fast as they could and tried to move around wrecks without slowing too much. Cooper watched behind them from his perch half out of the air vent on the roof of the camper. He had stacked cases of water and other solid items to stand on. Quinn was watching the front and sides for any trouble. They made good time but the ride felt endless with all of their nerves strung tight waiting for the bikers to catch up to them.

Quinn was looking back when he felt Dara start to slow the truck. He turned around and saw that they were approaching a roadblock. There were cars pulled across the road three deep and an old bus was in the center of it all. There were men on top of the bus, all armed and pointing their weapons at the lead truck and more behind the cars blocking the road.

Quinn yelled at Dara through the open window, "Stop about ten feet from the cars!"

He slung his gun behind his back and got ready to jump out. He hoped the guards weren't trigger happy and would give them a chance to explain. Quinn vaulted over the side of the truck bed down to the road and raised his hands. He started to walk forward to the front of the truck and stopped just past the driver's door. He wanted to be able to run back quickly if they started to shoot.

When no gunshots came and none of the guards made a greeting he yelled out to them.

"I'm looking for Sheriff McCormac!"

There was a brief pause while the guards talked to each other and then one man dropped down and appeared around a car and walked towards Quinn. When he was five feet away he stopped and scanned the three vehicles.

"Do I know you son? I'm the sheriff." he asked. He was tall and broad with a face that needed shaving but his uniform and hair were clean.

"No Sir, but we have something that belongs to you. My friends and I were attacked on the road by a biker gang and taken prisoner. We managed to escape and we brought a bunch of kids that were there with us. They say this is the town that they live in." Quinn told him.

A look of desperate hope crossed the man's face, "My son, Luke?" he almost begged.

"Yes Sir, he's with the others."

Before Quinn could explain further the Sheriff turned and waved at his men. "They've found Luke and the other kids! Get out here!" he yelled and turned back to Quinn. "Where are they?" he demanded as four guards rushed up to stand behind him.

"Sir we have to get inside. We killed the leader of the gang and some of his people and burned the place down but there were more that had left to get friends from your town. We hid on a side road until they passed us, then booked it here. They'll be after us by now for what we did. We need to get these kids into town before they get here." he said in desperation. He could feel the minutes slipping by.

"You killed Skull and burned his place down?" one of the guards asked skeptically.

A voice from behind him answered, "Yes we did, as well as two of his men and a woman. Now can we please get behind that road block and get the kids to safety?" Dara asked from the open window of the truck.

Quinn heard the sound of footsteps and turned to see Alex and Josh coming towards him. Cooper was still on the top of the camper scanning back down the road. He turned back to the Sheriff and his men. They all looked doubtful at Dara's statement. The Sheriff looked Alex and Josh over and glanced at Dara with a frown.

"So let me get this straight. A bunch of teenagers killed the leader of one of the worst biker gangs in the state, some of his men, rescued some kids and then burned their place to the ground? Is that what you're trying to tell me?" he asked sarcastically.

Josh stepped forward, "Yup, they had a basement full of drugs, like millions of dollars' worth and we couldn't leave that for their friends, so we torched the place. Sir, do you want your kids back or not?" he said in exasperation.

"Too late, they're here!" Cooper suddenly yelled from the top of the camper.

Dara jumped out of the truck and joined her friends as they all made their way back down the road towards the oncoming bikers. Over his shoulder, Quinn instructed the Sheriff.

"These guys aren't coming to talk Sheriff. Get your men ready!"

Josh stopped at the van and grabbed extra ammo clips for the rifles that they all were carrying. Cooper stayed up high and braced himself to start shooting. When he saw Dara, Alex, Josh and Quinn line up behind the camper he called advice down to them.

"Remember to keep your gun barrel down. It's going to keep going too high. Just stay calm and aim and spray. Remember what these guys were going to do to us and what they did to Luke and the kids. We're going to stop them from hurting anyone else."

Alex took a deep breath and steadied herself. She was surprised to see that her hands weren't shaking. She reminded herself how she felt hanging from the hooks and the emptiness in Luke's eyes. That was all she needed to harden her resolve for what she was about to do.

There were four bikes that roared up with each one carrying two men. They skidded to a stop twenty feet from the back of the camper and quickly jumped off. The biggest of the bunch roared at them.

"I'm gonna skin you alive for what you did to my friends!" as he pulled his sawed off shot gun from behind his back.

The rest of the gang fanned out in a line and they were all pulling guns when Quinn yelled out, "Fire!"

There was nothing pretty or accurate about the wave of bullets that swarmed towards the bikers. Many bullets hit the road and ricocheted up from the ground or went flying too high, but enough of the wall of fire hit their marks to completely slaughter the eight men facing the teens. The sound of automatic weapons was amazingly loud and it continued until all of their clips ran dry.

The silence that followed the shooting was almost as deafening. They all stood there staring at the massacred pile of bodies and it was then that Alex started to shake. It was the sound of a shot gun being cocked that brought them back to the real world.

Quinn dropped his weapon and raised his hands into the air as he turned to face the sheriff. The other teens followed his lead and did the same. Only Cooper kept his weapon and in the silence they could clearly hear a fresh clip being slammed home into his gun. The four standing on the road had all turned to face the Sheriff who was pointing his shot gun at them.

"Five teenagers with Ak47's just opened fire and killed eight men in front of the Law and you expect me to believe that you are the good guys?" he asked with shock on his face.

"Sir," Quinn began, but Alex cut him off.

"Eight men who were going to rape and kill me and my friends and who put a dog collar on your son and beat him!" she yelled at him, furious. "Luke! Luke your Dad's out here and he thinks we are the bad guys!" she yelled toward the van.

Sudden loud banging came from the inside of the van and a faint voice could be heard yelling, "Dad!" over and over. The look on the Sheriff's face changed from shock to uncertain.

His men had come up behind him and he looked over and said, "Cover them while I check this out."

He walked over to the vans rear door and unlatched it. He rolled it up and was immediately hit by a small flying bundle that wrapped itself around him. The Sheriff staggered back at the weight of the boy but his arms closed over him in reflex. Before he could speak, Luke started jabbering at him.

"Dad! Dad, Alex saved me. She saved all of us. She's a hero not a bad guy!"

"Luke? Oh God Luke! I thought I'd lost you." and he started to sob as he clutched the child to his chest.

One of the guards looked away from the reunion and lowered his gun. He looked at the kids with disbelief and asked, "Who are you kids?"

Of course it was Josh who answered in a pure Josh way, "We're the motherfucking Maple Leaf Mafia!"

His friends all groaned and laughed.

Chapter 14

The camper was set up in the town's campground, located in a park in the downtown area. There had been lots of offers given to the group for places to stay but they had all wanted some time alone so they chose the campground. It didn't stop people from coming by to thank them or just chat but it was away from the bulk of the town's population. They had had to tell their story again at the road block but it was the children that had convinced all the guards that the teens were their saviors. Once the children had seen the Sheriff and men they recognised, they had come to life and all started to talk at once. Once their status as "good guys" was confirmed, they were allowed into the town.

They followed the Sheriff, who was driving an ATV into the downtown area. Word spread fast about the rescued children and parents came running. There were tears and sobs of relief and many thank-you's and God bless you's for the teens.

Once all the children had been returned to their parents, it was decided that there would be a town party held later that night as a celebration. The town was in good shape thanks to the Sheriff and his men. They had a few old generators working and had water pumps going at different locations. They had kept strict control over the food stores and were rationing and planting as much seed as they could. They were lucky with the climate and could grow certain plants year round.

The group of teens had been very careful with their water and had only been hand washing themselves and their clothes but with a party on the schedule the girls wanted to clean up properly and wash their hair. The Sheriff sent the girls off with a local lady to the community center. They were using it as a central meeting place for the town and it had one of the precious generators hooked up to it so they had hot water for the gym's showers. The girls grabbed towels and toiletries and raced after the woman. They were so excited about having their first hot shower in six days.

The Sheriff stayed with the boys after handing his son off to his sobbing mother. He quizzed the boys on what they had seen on the way from Disneyland. He also wanted to talk to them about their automatic weapons. They had a few in town, but he would like to add to that number for the defence force he was building. The teens had decided not to tell anyone about how many guns they had taken from the basement.

All told they had carried out forty six Ak47 automatic rifles from the basement and forty cases of ammunition. It would make for very good barter and once they got home, they would have it for defence if things there were as bad off. After talking it over they had decided to give the Sheriff three of the guns and three cases of ammo as a goodwill gesture and for stocking them with more water and supplies when they left.

The kids wanted to stay in the town for a few days to let Josh's face heal. Both his eyes were swollen almost shut and his lips were both split. One of the town's doctors had come by and checked him out. Nothing was broken in his face so time would heal it.

After taking their luxurious, hot showers, the girls were delirious with happiness to discover blow dryers and curling irons in the change rooms. With the generator powering them they styled their hair and felt for a few minutes that things were back to normal. Alex kept expecting the ordeal they just faced to set in with some kind of shock but it never came. She talked to Dara about it while they did their hair.

"I'm feeling really weird that I'm not more upset about what we just went through." she explained to Dara.

Dara paused curling her hair with a thoughtful look on her face.

"I think what happened will always stay with us and we will all carry a dark place in our hearts for having to kill those people. But I also think what we did was right. Those people were evil. They enjoyed causing pain and torment and we stopped them from doing it ever again. Think about it this way, one hundred years ago, those types of people would have been executed on the spot. For decades now, criminals have been able to do whatever they wanted with very few consequences. Barely any jail time or maybe even none if they have a slick lawyer and even in jail it's us, the victims that really have to pay. We pay to feed and house them. I mean, they have better health care than a lot of people, not to mention food and TV. The death penalty is a joke. Twenty years after the crime and maybe they finally get executed. Why do they get to live a long time but their victim doesn't? It's not fair and it's so not justice. So I think the clock has been set back and now justice will finally be served. That's what today felt like to me Alex, justice. And I'll tell you something else, it felt right."

Alex thought about all the times she read news about bad guys getting off on a technicality or hardly even getting any jail time at all. She remembered hearing stories about victims being sued by criminals for different reasons and the bad guy winning; or repeat offenders doing the same crime again and again and being released from jail. Dara was right, justice was served today and Alex felt her spirit lift even more.

When the girls got back to the camper and trucks, the boys gave appreciative looks to the styled girls and Josh let off a wolf whistle. They were due at the party soon so the boys went for their own showers while the girls changed into clean clothes and watched over the vehicles. After the Sheriff had left, the boys had repacked the van with all the guns and ammo and used a pad lock to secure the latch. They didn't want to be stuck guarding it while they were in town. When the boys came back they were ready to go to the party. They left the machine guns locked up but all of them carried hand guns in holsters that they had picked up on their travels.

As they approached the town square, they could hear music from a band playing and smell the wonderful aroma of home cooked food. There were long tables set up around a cleared area for dancing. The biggest table was piled high with dishes of steaming food and as people arrived they would add whatever they had brought to it. Alex and Dara had made buns before they were captured by the gang and they were still in the grocery bags in a cupboard when they checked so they brought them to contribute.

The Sheriff waved them over to his table and they sat and dined with him and many of his deputies. They told their story over and over as people came by to greet them. With filled bellies they were all relaxed and having fun watching the dancers. The Sheriff was talking about the men who were with the bikers that came after the kids.

"We knew some of those guys from town but we didn't know they were working with Skull and his gang. When we went to their houses we found a lot of stolen and stock piled goods, as well as a ton of drugs and guns. They were probably telling him about our security set up so they could attack us at some point. You kids did a really good thing by burning that drug den down and killing them all. It will save us a lot of problems in the future."

A much cleaner Luke came running up and gave his Dad a hug, a cheeky smile to Alex and dashed off again to play with his friends.

"I can't thank you enough for bringing him back to us. His Mother, well, she was barely hanging on for the past few days." He turned away emotionally.

As the Sheriff was getting his composure back, a man walked up to the table that they hadn't met yet. He had a smile on his face as he looked the kids over but his eyes were cold. Alex felt herself shiver when he looked at her.

"Well, here's the heroes of the day! You must be a tough group of kids to take out Skull and his men. Yes Sir! You all did this community a great service by ridding us of them." he exclaimed in thanks, but the smile on his face never reached his eyes.

The Sheriff beamed at the man, "They sure did John." He replied turning to the teens. "This is my right hand man, John Harper. He's on the town council and helped us get organized and security set up after the lights went out. John, this is Quinn, Alex, Josh, Dara and Cooper. They brought my boy back and the other missing kids from the field trip. You probably heard that the biker gang had them."

John had been nodding as the Sheriff was speaking

"Yes and a great day it is to have our children home. I'd love to hear more about this great escape. Tell me kids, how did you manage to get off the wall hooks?"

Within seconds of him asking the question he had five guns pointed at him

The Sheriff shoved his chair back and jumped to his feet, "Whoa, whoa. What's going on here kids? Why are you pointing guns at John?" he asked frantically as his hand moved toward his holstered weapon.

Without taking her eyes off John, Alex answered him in a cold voice. "Because we never told anyone about the wall hooks they put us on. So the only way he would know is if the bikers told him or he's been in the place. Either way, it means he was working with them. Tell me John, did you know they had the children too?" Alex asked him in a disgusted voice.

The man was red in the face and tried to act surprised at the charges but it was clearly an act and he couldn't keep the hate from his eyes.

The music had stopped and in the silence everyone had heard Alex clearly. All of the townspeople were staring at the drama unfolding at the Sheriff's table and some had even drawn their weapons. The Sheriff was studying his friends face when he drew his weapon and turned it on him.

"Where were you this afternoon John? I sent a man to your place and you weren't home. With all the excitement I figured you would show up. Where were you?" he asked in a harsh voice.

"I'll tell you where he was." Dara spoke up. "He went with the guys from town out to the house we burnt down. You went to join the party didn't you? They told you they had a couple of young girls strung up on the wall, hanging from hooks and you went out to have some fun. And when you found the place burnt down you hung back while your friends chased after us. That's what happened, isn't it?" she was yelling by the time she ended.

The man turned to the Sheriff in desperation, "You have to believe me! I just went to try and get them free. I was negotiating with Skull to get the children back. I never would have hurt them. I was trying to help the town!" he pleaded, looking around at the confused and angry faces.

The Sheriff grabbed a bunch of John's shirt, bunching it up and yanked him face to face. "You knew where my son was? All along, while Jane and I were frantic and you knew where he was? You were with us when we found the empty bus and watched as we grieved. You knew he was being kept like a dog with a collar on his neck and being beaten and you let us weep?" He threw the sniveling man away from him.

"You were my friend!" he roared in disbelief just as a shot rang out. John Harper crumpled to the ground face first and there was a large bloody hole in his back. Standing behind him with her gun still raised was Luke's mother, Jane.

She looked to her husband and stated simply, in a calm voice "They burnt my baby's skin with cigarettes." and then she turned and walked away. The crowd parted for her and when she was gone everyone started talking at once. The Sheriff scrubbed his hands across his face and turned to the kids.

"Thank you again. I think the party is over." and he followed his wife out.

Alex motioned to her friends, "Let's go guys. I'm tired and just want to sleep."

They went back to the camper and decided that they would need to stand watches after all. There might be more people in town that had worked for the bike gang.

After the excitement of the first night the kids enjoyed the next three days of peace. They took stock of their supplies and repacked them for easier access. They had decided to take the van with them in case one of the other vehicles broke down they would still have two. They traded the guns and ammunition to the Sheriff for things that they didn't have and took as many hot showers as they could. They knew that once they left, it would be back to sponge baths and boiled water. By the third day, Josh's face was a rainbow of colours but most of the swelling had gone down so he could see better. It had been nine days since they left Disneyland and they were all anxious to keep heading homeward.

Alex couldn't help thinking of Emily and David and wondering how far they had come and if they were safe. She tried hard not to think of her family and all the "what ifs" or she would sink into depression. They planned to leave the next morning as early as possible to take advantage of the daylight and get as far as they could. The days were getting longer but the sun still went down before seven at night and they wanted to push hard after staying in the town for three days.

They had dinner at the Sheriff's house the night before they left and they were all happy to see Luke full of energy and happiness. With the resilience of young children, he seemed to be none the worse for his ordeal. The physical scars on his small body would take time to heal but his mental state seemed good. His mother, Jane, was a charming hostess and bustled around mothering all the teens. She seemed not to be effected by the fact that she had shot a man in the back only days ago

Alex remembered what Dara had said in the change room, about a return to the old ways and guessed that it really would be a new world. They left the Sheriff's house feeling good about what was to come and went to bed early for the next leg of their trip home.

Chapter 15

Six days later, Alex was happy to see the mountains of Montana after taking so long to get through Idaho. They had left the town and cut through the north western corner of Utah with no problems. They tried to stay away from towns as much as possible and Idaho made that easy with its low population. Of the six days they had traveled since leaving the town, two of the days were spent in frustrating back tracking. Some roads had been impossible to get around car crashes and at one point they saw homemade sign's warning traveller's to turn back or be shot. They didn't want to get into another fight so they turned back and searched for another route. Local maps were getting hard to find as it seemed that all the gas stations they stopped at had been looted. The group did see other people but not as many as in the first few days.

On the second day they saw a woman pushing a stroller down the side of the road and stopped to offer her a ride. She was very suspicious and clutched a small pistol in her hand. When Dara told her she could ride alone with her, the woman relaxed and was very friendly. Her baby was under a year old and she had been stuck in a bigger town that she had gone shopping at. They had stayed as long as they could with friendly strangers but food was tight and she wanted to go home.

They gave her fresh baked buns and water and dropped her off outside of her town. The group had discussed helping people, especially people with children when they could but all agreed that avoiding people was better. Not all the people they stopped to help were nice.

In southern Idaho they saw a man walking with two boys and they stopped to offer a ride. The two boys were skinny and dirty and didn't speak. The man took in the three working vehicles with calculation and envy. He accepted the ride and they climbed into the camper.

Alex was driving with Josh taking a turn keeping watch out of the roof vent. Alex tried to engage the man in conversation but he just answered her questions with grunts. She could see him in the rear view mirror, taking in all the supplies piled up in the rear of the camper. He kept taking quick looks at Josh's legs braced on the water cases.

Alex had a bad feeling about the guy and wondered about the silent boys. She'd given them juice boxes and more of the buns that they kept stockpiling. The boys ate in small bites with their heads down. She was getting nervous about the way the man kept checking on Josh's position. She eased her hand gun out of its holster and set it on her lap. They had been driving in silence for twenty minutes when the man made his move.

He stood up from the dinette table and stretched. As soon as she saw him in the mirror take a step towards her, she tapped the brakes twice and grabbed her gun, keeping it down on her lap. He came in a rush and got right beside her. There was a small revolver in his hand and he pointed it at her side. He was trying to hide what he was doing if Josh came down into the camper.

In a normal tone of voice, like they were just having a conversation he told her, "I don't think it's really fair that you kids have three working cars. That seems very greedy to me so I think you should give me one. At the next side road I want you to turn off and give it some gas. We're going to ditch your friends and then when we are safely away I'll let you and your friend go."

Alex didn't know if the man was blind or just stupid. He didn't seem to remember the assault rifle that Josh had in his hands when he was on the roof or the two guns Alex had strapped to her waist. He was seriously out gunned.

"That's not going to happen, Mister. How about I pull over and let you leave my camper alive instead?" and she nodded downwards. With her right hand on the wheel she had the gun in her left hand and her arm was across her stomach which meant that the gun's barrel was inches from his ribs.

The man looked down and paled a bit but his resolve hardened, "Put that away little girl. You know you aren't going to shoot me in front of those boys." he ordered.

"I wouldn't mess with her Mister. That "little girl" snapped the neck of a biker with nothing but her thighs and if she doesn't take care of you, I will!" Josh told him. He had come up behind the stranger, alerted by Alex's braking pattern.

The man slumped in defeat when he felt the barrel of Josh's gun against the back of his head. He whined "I wasn't going to hurt you. I just want the camper. It's not fair that you kids have three vehicles!"

Josh ignored the whining man and plucked the gun from his hand.

"Alex, toot the horn twice and put your signal light on. Pull over and we'll get rid of this trash."

Josh grabbed the man by the collar and pulled him back onto his butt, then dragged him back towards the side door. Alex pulled over and put the camper in park. She slid out of her seat and went into the back of the camper. She looked at the two boys and felt bad for them.

"I'm sorry boys. You're going to have to go back to walking with your Dad." she told them.

Neither boy had even looked up at the commotion but the older boy mumbled something. Alex thought that he looked around eight or nine. She crouched down beside him and asked "What did you say sweetie?"

The boy finally looked up into Alex's eyes and she was shocked to see that they were full of rage. "I said he's not our Dad! We don't even know him and he's an asshole!" the child said with force.

The pathetic man on the floor yelled at the kid, "Shut up you ungrateful little shit!"

Josh poked him with the rifle barrel to shut him up.

"Tell me what happened, sweetie." Alex asked the boy gently.

His eyes welled up and his little brother started to cry. "My Mom was driving us to school and we had a crash. I couldn't wake her up. I tried all day!" he cried out. Then in a whisper, "I think she was dead."

"I'm so sorry honey. There were a lot of car crashes that day." She gently rubbed his back. "How did you end up with this man?"

The boy looked over at the man with fierce eyes. "No one came. All day we waited for help and we were hungry and scared. When it was getting dark, he came and made us go with him. He said we had to pretend that he was our Dad because people would help us if they thought he had kids. He said he would beat us if we spoke to anyone. And he hit my brother lots of times to make him be quiet. He's a really bad man. He robbed some people that were going to give us food. And they kicked us out of a shelter when they caught him stealing stuff. Please don't make us go with him. We will be really good and quiet if we can stay with you guys." he pleaded.

The camper door was thrown open just then and Cooper and Quinn were standing outside with their guns pointed in.

"What's going on?" Quinn asked, eyeing the snivelling man on the floor.

"We're just getting ready to throw out some trash." Josh joked and shoved the man out the door. Quinn jumped back and the man hit the pavement hard. "Off you go buddy. We'll take care of the kids from here."

He scrambled to his feet and whined. "My gun, please can I have my gun back. It's dangerous out here. I need to be able to protect myself.

"That's funny. It sounds like you just said something but that can't be right because dead men don't talk." Josh said in an amused tone that turned menacing. "Start walking or I'll start shooting." He lifted his gun to his shoulder and took aim.

"Fine, fine I'll go! The little brats were too much work anyways. You can keep them." The man jumped and took off running when Quinn shot the ground at his feet. Josh looked to him with a grin.

"What?" Quinn asked with a shrug. "I've always wanted to do that."

Alex rolled her eyes "Can we go now, please."

After getting as much information as they could from the two boys about other family members they checked the map and found that their Grandparents lived in a town that was only forty miles out of the way. They drove the boys to the town and handed them off to the guards at a roadblock with promises from the guards to get the boys to their family.

Alex and Dara handed out buns to them all. The camper always smelled like fresh baked buns as the girls made them nonstop. They found that the buns made a great goodwill gesture and it smoothed a lot of tension with the people they ran into. Having a good amount of flour and baking supplies from Mr. Peterson's house they felt it was more than worth it to give buns away. They each knew how lucky they were to have transportation and supplies and felt it was a small thing to do to give back.

They were getting closer to the Montana border the next day when they heard gunshots. Quinn was on the roof of the camper and Cooper was in the back of the truck on guard. They couldn't see where the gunfire was coming from but Quinn caught sight of sparks flying off the top of the van on the driver's side so he knew they were the target. Quinn let loose with his automatic rifle and poured bullets into the bush on the left hand side of the road. Cooper followed suit and they kept it up until their clips ran dry. Alex was driving the truck in the lead and she sped up, trying to get out of range. Once they had gone around a few bends and put some distance between themselves and the shooters she slowed down.

It was a few hours later that they came upon an old antique school bus parked on the road beside three abandoned cars. They came up slowly and came to a stop fifty feet behind it. With the wrecked cars on one side and the bus in the middle of the road, there wasn't room to safely go around. Quinn saw an older man stand up from one of the wrecked cars when he heard their engines. He had a shot gun in his hands but it was pointing at the road. He scanned the three vehicles and seemed to make up his mind. He smiled, gave a wave and placed his gun on the top of the car he was standing by.

The kids were still a little on edge after being shot at earlier so Quinn and Cooper went forward alone with their guns, armed and ready. As they came closer the man almost seemed to recognize them. He had a big grin on his face when he greeted them.

"Well hello! I didn't think I'd run into you kids out here on the road. It's good to see you! Can you give me a hand? Some cotton pickin' yahoos shot at me down the road and thankfully they had really bad aim. All they hit was my spare gas cans. I'm trying to siphon some gas to get these folks to the end of my route." and waved at the bus.

Quinn and Cooper looked towards the bus and saw a bunch of faces peering out at them. Turning back to the old man with a frown Quinn asked, "Sir, you seem to think you know us but I don't think we've met. Who are you?"

"Oh where did my manners go? I'm Jasper Welch. I'm very pleased to meet you." he offered his hand in greeting. "You're those Canadian kids aren't you?" he asked while shaking the boys' hands.

Quinn and Cooper look at each other in bafflement.

"Yup, heard all about you kids. I've been driving old Gertie back and forth, shuttling people ever since the lights went out so I hear all kinds of news. You kids are almost famous for takin' out that gang in Nevada. Say, you don't happen to have any of those buns do you?"

Shaking his head in amazement, Cooper headed back to the camper to get buns and tell the others about the new legend they had become. Quinn stayed and helped the man fill up his jerry cans that had been repaired with duct tape.

They exchanged information about the best roads ahead and told each other their respective stories. After Quinn corrected some of the wilder details of the biker battle that the man had been told, they finished up with the gas cans and strapped them back on the bus.

"So what made you turn bus driver Mr. Welch?" Quinn asked.

"Well, I used to drive old Gertie here in parades and for special functions for fun but after everything quit working, I was worried about getting enough food so I opened me a bussing business. Depending on how far someone wants to go, is how many cans of food I charge. I don't have a lot of competition." he laughed and slapped his knee. "And for the first time since I was a young fella gas is real affordable!"

Quinn couldn't help laughing with the good humoured man. Alex walked up carrying two grocery bags of buns and with a grin at the man said "I hear an order has been placed for our famous buns." She handed them over to the man. "Now you share those out with your passengers, don't keep them all for yourself." she teased.

"Well aren't you the sweetest thing! It's a real pleasure to see such goodness in this new world we're in. I sure hope you all make it home." He nodded at Quinn and Alex and made his way back to his old bus.

They stood there watching the bus drive away. Quinn had to laugh "No phones, no internet and no TV and we manage to make the news in at least three states. What are the odds?"

Alex looked at him deadpan and said "Well, I do make really good buns. Word was bound to spread." And she walked away.

** ** ** ** ** ** ** ** **

Crossing the border into Montana had everyone excited. They were almost back to Canada and so much closer to their homes and families. They were two hours into Montana when shots rang out again. Dara was driving the truck this time with Quinn in the back keeping guard.

It was uncomfortable riding guard duty but the boys insisted they do it with the girls driving. They rotated positions every few hours to keep themselves fresh.

The shots came from the right hand side and Josh, who was on the camper look out, sprayed the area with bullets. Cooper was driving the van in the middle of the caravan and he saw Quinn go flying sideways down into the truck bed. He honked his horn again and again and sped up right on the trucks tail. Dara took the hint and hit the gas, quickly pulling away. Josh didn't know if he hit the attackers but they stopped firing while he was spraying the area. They were speeding down the road faster than normal and Josh kept low in case there were more attackers. When they had gone ten minutes with no shots being fired at them, he felt the camper slow and start to pull over. He couldn't see the truck with the van in front of them but he knew something was wrong when he hadn't heard Quinn's gun firing.

He stayed up in position, scanning the area for any threats while they stopped. When he heard Dara screaming for the first aid kit, his heart took a painful stutter. He knew Quinn had been hit. He kept watch over his friends and prayed.

Chapter 16

Alex's heart was pounding as she tore through the camper's storage area for the first aid kit. It had to be Quinn. If Dara was yelling and Cooper was driving, it had to be Quinn who was shot. Her hands finally landed on the white box with the Red Cross on it and she ripped it from the cupboard. A mantra of "He's ok, he's ok" kept playing through her mind as she rushed out and around the van. She climbed up into the back of the truck and froze.

"So much blood, how can there be so much blood?" was all she could think.

Dara was only wearing her bra. Her t-shirt was wadded up and pressed to Quinn's leg. Cooper was struggling with Quinn's belt, trying to get it free from around his waist. It finally pulled out of the last loop and Cooper slid it around Quinn's upper thigh, pulling it tight.

Alex could see that Dara was yelling, her face white and full of panic, but Alex couldn't hear her. She couldn't hear anything. She was lost in pain. She saw the serious little face of Quinn sitting on his Grandpa's tractor when they first met. She saw the time she had caught a huge fish and Quinn was there, giving her a huge grin and hug. She saw Quinn in the stands cheering so loudly for her when she won her first gymnastics meet and so many other times that he was there for her. It wasn't until he opened his eyes and lifted his head, looking straight into her eyes and trying to give her a reassuring smile that the world snapped back into focus and her hearing returned.

"Alex, give me the fucking case!" was the first thing she heard. Dara was yelling at her for the first aid kit.

Alex stepped forward and dropped to her knees beside Dara. She quickly flipped the case open and pulled out thick squares of gauze. Dara snatched them from her hand and replaced her blood soaked t-shirt with them. Alex reached over and placed her fingers against Quinn's throat, checking his pulse. She could feel his heart racing. In a complete turnaround from her panic attack, she felt herself settle and go calm.

In an authoritative voice she addressed everyone. "Alright, everyone settle down! Quinn, Quinn open your eyes and look at me!" He had his eyes squeezed shut in pain but at her tone, he opened them. "Ok, I know it looks bad and it hurts like crazy but you need to calm down. It's far from your heart and you will be just fine after we bandage you up. You need to get your heart rate down. So just breathe deep and try and calm yourself. Dara, change that gauze and then wrap his leg with the tension bandage. Not too tight! Cooper, good thinking with the belt, we need to move him into the camper and then get somewhere we can take a good look at him so let's move this stuff out of the way and slide him out the back. Do you think you can carry him or should we get Josh?"

"I can put him over my shoulder and get him to the camper if you'll hold his leg still."

They jumped down and moved supplies out of the way making a path to the end of the truck to slide Quinn out. Dara finished wrapping his leg and helped slide him from behind. They tried to keep his injured leg as steady as possible but he still let out groans of pain and they could see he was clenching his teeth against screaming. Cooper pulled Quinn over his shoulder in a fireman's carry and Alex tried to keep the leg still. Quinn was a big guy and Alex was surprised at Cooper's strength, carrying him to and up into the camper. They laid him on the floor and Alex was scared to see that he had passed out from the pain. Josh ducked down from the roof and went white at the sight of his unconscious and bloody friend.

"What are we going to do?" he asked the other three. They all looked to Alex and she tried not to panic.

"We need to find a house or a store that we can look at his leg properly. Better yet, a town with a doctor. Grab the map and let's see where we are."

"Alex, I already know. We are hours from anything. We picked this route so we wouldn't be anywhere near a town, remember? I don't think he can wait three hours for us to get him to a town that might not even have a doctor and where we might end up in a fight for the trucks and supplies we have." Dara told her in desperation.

Alex thought hard about what to do. She was so scared for her friend. They were on their own. "Ok let's brace him with pillows and blankets to keep him warm. We need to go. Dara, watch for a place to stop. It's the best thing we can do for now."

Cooper and Dara grabbed pillows and sleeping bags while Alex checked the gauze. It was spotted but the bleeding had slowed. She helped cover him up and then they all went back to their vehicles.

As Alex followed the truck and van she kept an eye on Quinn in the mirror. He was so pale and dark circles were already forming under his eyes. Her hands shook on the steering wheel at the thought of losing him. He was one of her best friends and even though there had never been any romantic moments between them, Alex always felt it was there under the friendship just waiting to develop. She was still unsure about her feelings for Cooper. There had been many times on this trip when she had caught him looking at her that made her stomach flip in confusion, but the possibility of a future without Quinn made her even more unsure of how she felt.

They had been traveling for thirty minutes with nothing to see but forest when Dara slowed down and turned off the road they were traveling on. They went for five minutes before she turned again into a long driveway and through a pair of gates with a sign that read Griffin's Veterinary Services. The driveway opened up into cleared land with three beautiful buildings on it. They were made of river rock and weathered wood that suited the natural setting perfectly. The first building was the vet's office with a matching barn behind it and the third was a house further up the hill with a wraparound porch.

After scanning the area and seeing no one, Josh dropped down into the camper and stepped over Quinn, who was still unconscious.

"Sit tight Alex. I want to check the building for anyone before we move him." he was out the door and racing towards the office before Alex could reply.

Cooper joined him and they both went into the building with guns raised. They were back in minutes with a stretcher. Dara met them at the camper and Josh told them "It's empty but for the love of God, don't open the door in the back! There must have been no one here since it happened because there are dead animals in cages back there and it doesn't look or smell very pretty. There's an exam room with big windows so it's got lots of light. Let's get him in there and take a look at his leg. I want to check out the house and make sure it's empty."

The two boys went into the camper with the stretcher but the girls stayed outside to give them more room. It was tight and awkward in the confines of the camper and they realized right away they wouldn't be able to take him out the side door on the stretcher. They had to keep it straight out the door and move Quinn on to it. If Quinn had been awake, he would have been screaming in pain from all the jostling of his body but they got him on the stretcher and out of the camper. Alex rushed ahead and held the door for them.

There was a slight stench of rotting bodies but Alex had smelled a lot worse living on a farm. There was a light coating of dust on all the surfaces telling her that no one had been here since the lights went out. The exam room was bright with natural light from the two big windows but not as bright as it would have been with the fluorescent lights on.

They left Quinn on the stretcher and put the whole thing on the large exam table. Dara grabbed a pair of scissors and started cutting up Quinn's cargo pant leg so they wouldn't have to try and wrestle them off of him. Alex unwound the tension bandage and removed the gauze padding. Dara cut the rest of the pant leg away but there was so much blood they couldn't see the bullet wound. Alex looked around the room and saw a bottle of sterilized water on a counter with drawers and cupboard under it.

She grabbed the water and poured it slowly over the bloody area. He had been shot on the outside of his thigh. Once the leg was clean and they could see the wound, she stepped back.

"Oh shit." she whispered. Quinn didn't have a bullet wound, he had two. She looked at her friends and saw Dara crying and shaking. Cooper and Josh were both pale and looked helplessly at Quinn's leg.

She took a deep breath and said, "There's no exit wounds, both bullets are still in his leg."

Josh turned and left the room for a moment, when he returned he told them "There's two holes in the side of the truck. He was shot through the wood so it would have slowed them down. They can't stay in his leg or he'll die of infection. Someone has to take them out."

Alex looked at the others but they were all looking at her.

"Me? You want me to operate on him? Are you crazy?" she said in panic.

"Well, you've got some training and you said you want to be a doctor so you're the best one to do it." Josh told her.

Alex just stared at him in disbelief. "What training? I volunteer at a senior's home! I change bed pans and feed them applesauce! I have no training, and yeah I want to be a doctor one day but that's in like, ten years!"

"Come on Alex, you're always watching that show on TLC about operating and what about that other show you love? You know the one with McStinky or whatever his name is? You're the closest thing we have to a doctor here. Quinn needs you." Josh argued.

Alex shook her head, "It's a TV show Josh, not medical school. Just because I watch Grey's Anatomy doesn't mean I'm Christina Yang! Seriously, seriously?" only Dara got the reference and gave a small snort of laughter. She stepped over to Alex and put her hand on her arm.

"I'm sorry Alex. I can't do it. I'm ready to puke just looking at his leg. I don't do well with blood."

Alex nodded in understanding and look at the two boys. Josh was shaking his head. He held up his big hands, "Look at these Alex. Do you really think I should stick these big suckers in to Quinn's leg? Give me a hammer and I'll pound something for you but not this, sorry."

Alex huffed out in frustration. He was right. She looked to Cooper who was already backing away.

"Oh no, not me! I'll steal you an operating room but I can't work in one!"

Alex glared at him in disgust. She knew by now that his bad boy reputation was a sham and that he was a really good guy.

"Damn it!" she stomped her foot in frustration. "You know who could do this? He could!" she pointed to Quinn who was starting to come around.

When he groaned in pain, she knew she didn't have a choice. Alex glared at her friends and started barking out orders. "We need to get supplies. This place should have everything we need. Cooper, look for a drug cabinet. He's going to need something stronger than Aspirin. Josh, look for surgery stuff. Scalpels, sponges, clamps, retractors and stuff like that. I'm not sure how to use that stuff but we should have it here. You've seen stuff on TV and in movies too. We're all going to pretend we know what we're doing. Dara find reference books, like drug dosage and operating books. Maybe we'll get lucky and find a manual." she joked sarcastically.

It was easier for Alex to be mad than scared of what she was about to do, so while her friends scattered through the building she started to rip open drawers and cupboards angrily.

"Alex?" a hoarse voice asked behind her.

She whirled around and saw Quinn looking at her in confusion. "Where are we?" he asked.

Alex went to him and held his hand. "We found a veterinarian's office. How are you feeling?"

"It hurts, feels like my leg is on fire. How bad is it?"

"You were shot twice. The bullets went through the wooden sides of the truck bed wall so they slowed down enough to not go through. Both bullets are still in your leg." She took a deep breath and told him "I'm going to take them out."

He gave her a faint smile, "Good. If you're going to be a doctor one day, you'll need the practice."

She gave a half laugh "Oh God, Quinn, I'm so scared! I don't know if I can do this." Tears started to run down her cheeks as she bowed her head, all of her defensive anger gone.

His hand tightened hard on hers and she looked into his eyes. "You can do this. I trust you with everything. Remember back when we were twelve and that fool of a dog, Duster, broke his leg? You splinted it up with a stick and my T-Shirt and made me carry him back to the farm from the back field. You were like a little General barking orders, you were so sure of yourself. You need to be like that now. I believe in you Alex."

"Oh Quinn, that was nothing like this! I'm going to have to cut your leg open to get those bullets out. It's so not the same." she almost wailed.

"I believe in you Alex." Quinn said again. "But before you start, do you think I could have a Tylenol?" he tried a joke to cheer her up.

Dara came back into the room with two thick books, "Got it Alex. The top one is a reference guide to different medications and dosage charts by weight. The bottom one has different minor surgeries on animals. There's a section on bullet wounds. I don't know if it will help but take a look anyway. Hey Quinn, ready to be Alex's guinea pig?"

Alex snatched the books and started to look up different pain killers. She didn't want Quinn to feel what she was about to do to him. She set it aside when she realized that she needed to see what Cooper found in the drug cabinet first. The other heavy text book had a bookmark at 'Gunshot wounds' and she started to pour over it. There were sections for dogs, cows, horses and other animals. It was a basic guide to bullet removal and directed the reader to other texts for more invasive procedures. Alex was happy to have some guidance but knew there was a big difference between a dog and a human.

Josh came in pushing a rolling cart piled high with packages, linens and a few different bottles. "Hey Alex, there's a supply closet that has a ton of stuff in it. It even has a bunch of these packages with sterilized instruments ready to go. There's disinfectant and scrubs and surgery drapes. Look this stuff over and see if there's anything missing." He was pleased at his find and gave a big grin.

Alex was still pissed off that she had been nominated to do the surgery so she barely looked up from the text book when she said "Right. Great. Thanks. Now go boil some water."

Josh didn't seem to mind her attitude and gave her a salute with a quick "On it boss!" as he rushed back out.

Cooper came in with a pan full of bottles and plastic wrapped syringes. "Sorry it took so long, the door was locked and I had to get the crowbar to open it. There are some painkillers that I recognise and some antibiotics, I think. Their names end in 'cillin' so I'm guessing that they are a type of penicillin. I grabbed some needles too but I have no idea how much you would dose him with."

Again, Alex didn't look up just pointed to the counter beside her. They all kept saying things like "Alex's guinea pig" and "what you need" and "you would dose him" and the pressure of responsibility was squeezing tighter. She tried to focus on the dosage chart but had to turn and ask Quinn "How much do you think you weigh Quinn?"

He opened his pain filled eyes and told her "Around one eighty, I think. Why, did you find me some good drugs Alex?" he asked hopefully.

It was too much. It was all just too much for her to handle. She gave him a tight smile, "Yup. Be right back." and turned and fled the room. She hit the front door running and whipped around the side of the building. Alex came to an abrupt stop and doubled over puking her guts out. She heaved painfully until there was nothing left in her stomach. She stayed bent over with her arms hugging herself while she sobbed.

She just wanted to go home. She was only sixteen, just a kid. It wasn't fair. She had been hung from a wall to be raped. She had shot and killed people and now she was supposed to perform surgery on one of her best friends. Why did this have to happen to her? She just wanted her Mom and Dad. She wanted to go home.

When her sobs subsided, she stood back up and looked out over the fields. The voice behind her didn't jolt her but the words did.

"There's a reason why we all think you should be the one to do this Alex. You're our leader. You always have been. Right back to when we were kids and you marched us into the forest and bossed us around to build our clubhouse. You've always taken the lead. Quinn might be the responsible one but you are our glue. It was always you that held us together and organised all the adventures growing up. You have the biggest heart and you are one of the strongest people I know. I wasn't surprised a bit when you came through that door at the biker's house. I knew you'd find a way to get free. You're a hero Alex. We trust you to do this."

Alex shook her head in denial, "I'm scared out of my mind Josh! I'm not a hero!"

He smiled a compassionate smile, "Don't you know Alex? That's what a hero is. Someone who's scared out of their mind and does it anyway." He opened his arms wide and she rushed into them. He held her tight and said no more.

After a few minutes he pulled back and gave her the trademark devil grin of his. "I brought you something." and he pulled a bottle of rum from his back pocket. "Cooper grabbed it from that grocery store, remember? A little bit of liquid courage to steady your nerves."

Alex took the bottle and studied it thoughtfully and then shrugged. "What the hell. It sure can't hurt." and she took a big gulp. Josh howled with laughter when her face turned bright red and she started to wheeze. In a choking voice she said "As they say in the movies, let's do this!" and they both went back in to help their friend.

Chapter 17

When Alex and Josh entered the exam room, she was surprised to see the changes that Dara and Cooper had made. It actually looked semi-professional. Quinn was covered in a blue linen drape except for his wounded area. The rolling cart was beside the table and a row of gleaming instruments were resting on a clean towel. There was a brown bottle and an open package of sutures waiting as well. On the counter were two steaming basins of water with more towels and a box of latex gloves.

Cooper was wearing scrubs and holding another set. He stepped forward and addressed her in a professional voice "Ready to scrub in Doctor, I'll be assisting you for this procedure." as he handed her the clothing.

Alex took the outfit with a grateful smile to both of them for their help and slipped it on over her clothes. She went to the hot water and scrubbed her hands and arms with soap. Cooper used a cup and rinsed her arms over the sink so the rinse water would stay fresh for him. He handed her a towel and helped her put on the gloves. Alex looked at him in surprise for his no nonsense manner.

"What? I watch TV too. If you can't make it, fake it, right?" he said defensively.

Alex grinned at him and stepped back to give Dara room to help him with the rinsing of his hands. Alex went to the bottles of drugs and quickly did the math from the dosage chart and Quinn's weight. She filled a syringe with the amount of morphine she would need and turned to the exam table. Quinn was still awake but his face was full of pain and very pale. He was taking in all the activity in the room and smiled at Alex when he saw the needle she was holding.

"Gimmee!" he joked.

She laughed softly. The rum was spreading through her body and she was feeling stronger. "Are you sure you're ready for this?"

"Oh yeah, you can do anything you want to me after you give me the joy juice, Alex." His face turned serious. "Really Alex, I believe in you. You can do this. Like you said, it's a long way from my heart, right?"

"Ok, night-night then."

As she was about to stick Quinn in the arm with the needle, Josh interrupted.

"Wait! That's the right amount isn't it? You don't want to give him too much, right?"

Alex froze in place and closed her eyes in exasperation. She took a breath and in a flat voice replied, "I don't know Josh because I'm not a doctor and he's not a fucking DOG!" she spat the last word at him and tried to calm back down. "The book said this is the dosage for his weight so that's the best I can do. OK?"

Josh looked down at his feet and mumbled, "Okay, just checking. Sorry."

Alex sighed, "No, it's ok. I'm just nervous."

She turned back to Quinn and quickly slid the needle into his arm and pressed the plunger. Within minutes his eyes went hazy and started to droop. He mumbled some words that Alex thought were "That's the ticket." but she was unsure because they were slurred. She waited a few more minutes and then tried to wake him up.

When he didn't respond she grabbed the bottle of disinfectant and sprayed the wounded area, spreading it around with a sponge so his leg was covered. She turned to the cart and looked at the instruments on it. There were a couple of wicked sharp scalpels, large tweezers, a small spreader and other things she had no idea about. Cooper gave her a nod and she picked up the scalpel.

Her whole body tensed as she made a small cut on either side of the first bullet wound. Right away, she knew she would have to cut deeper to see where the bullet was. Cooper was right beside her with sponges and water. When she cut, he would pour sterilized water into the area and mop up the blood. Alex set aside the knife and grabbed the tweezers and spreader. She spread the wound open and once Cooper had mopped it up she could see the bullet. She got a grip on it and pulled it out. It wasn't very deep and she didn't think it had done much damage but she had no way of really knowing with no medical training. Nothing seemed to be gushing from the site so she took that as a good sign and removed the spreader and covered it with gauze. She would save the stitching for when she had both bullets out. The second bullet wasn't as deep as the first one but when she grabbed it with the tweezers something seemed to come out with it.

"Pour water on that Cooper. I don't know what it is and I don't want to pull it out until I do." she told him.

As the water cleared away she studied the object stuck with the bullet in the tweezers. "What is that? Hey Josh can you shine a flashlight on this please?" she asked him. Seconds later it was Cooper that identified it.

"It's a piece of his pants! The bullet must have taken in it into the hole. We need to check the other hole and make sure there isn't any more or he'll get infected. Go ahead and pull it out Alex."

She pulled it out and probed around in the wound for anything else that was loose but found nothing. Then she took out the spreader and went back to the first hole and checked it but it seemed free of any foreign objects.

"Ok, I think that's it. Should I pour more disinfectant into the holes or just sew them up?" When no one answered her she sighed "Damn it, where's Google when you need it!" She stared around the room trying to decide and her glance took in the bottles of drugs on the counter.

"I'm just going to sew him up and pump him full of antibiotics." and reached for the needle and suture thread.

It was a lot harder to sew skin than it was to sew cloth and she felt her stomach lurch every time she penetrated his skin with the needle. She put ten small stiches in one wound and eight in the other. Dara had thick bandages of gauze ready and she had smeared antibiotic ointment over them. After dressing the wounds and cleaning the blood off of Quinn as best they could, Alex consulted the drug book and gave him a shot of antibiotics.

She peeled her gloves and bloody scrubs off and dropped them in the garbage. She looked at her pale friend and could see the steady rise and fall of his chest as he slept. Her friends were all smiling at her and she had to grin back. They had done it. They had done their best and only time would tell if it was the right thing to do.

"Hey Josh, I really need something from you."

"Sure Alex, what do you need? Name it and it's yours."

"I need that bottle of rum!"

When he pulled it out of his back pocket and held it out, she went towards him and snatched from his hand as she sailed out the door. When he went looking for her later, he found the bottle empty and her asleep.

** ** ** ** ** ** ** ** ** ** **

When Alex woke up, she came up in a rush and banged her head hard. "ARGGGG!" her head was pounding and not just from banging it. Her mouth was paste dry and tasted like something had died in it. She remembered operating on Quinn and then sitting on a stump by the fence and drinking rum. She had never been much of a drinker, just one here and there at a party so she realized that she was experiencing her first hang over and vowed that it would be her last.

It was dark wherever she was so she felt around with her hands and figured out that she was in one of the bunks in the camper. She swung her legs over the side of the bunk and groaned again from the pain in her head. Water, she needed water and drugs, lots of drugs. She made her way to the tiny kitchen and grabbed a water bottle from the counter, she could barely see but after eight days of living in the camper she knew her way around in the dark. Opening a small cupboard she fumbled around until she found the bottle of aspirin and clutched it to her chest like a lifeline. She made her way to the side door and went outside.

It was either very late or very early and it wasn't until she looked to the east and she saw just a hint of lighter sky that she knew she had slept the rest of the afternoon and night away in drunken stupor. She shook her head at her own stupidity, causing it to pound even harder and making her stomach rush up her throat. She rushed away to the side of the vet office and vomited up the last of the rum.

"I guess that's the designated puking spot. Twice in twenty four hours, Alex? Nothing will ever grow there again!" Josh teased her from behind.

Her stomach felt better but her head was still killing her and she fumbled with the child proof cap on the painkillers. Josh plucked it from her hands and popped the lid off, handing her two pills. After rinsing her mouth with water she took the pills gratefully and downed them.

"How's Quinn? Did he wake up? Why are you awake? Where is everyone?" she fired at him.

Josh threw his head back and laughed "And she's back! God, I love you Alex."

"Yeah, yeah, I love you too, you big goof. Now answer my questions."

When he got his laughter under control he told her, "Quinn's fine. He woke up after about four hours and we fed him some soup. He didn't puke it up like you, so we took that as a good sign. He has no fever and his wounds are still dry and clean so it's a wait and see thing. We gave him some codeine pills and that made him so happy he went back to sleep and is still out. I'm up because we have a druggie and a drunk in our group and someone needs to keep watch while everyone is asleep." he finished with a raised eyebrow at her.

Alex looked at her feet in embarrassment. "Right, umm, good, I mean umm, oh crap. I'm sorry Josh. It was a really stupid thing to do. I'm sorry I left you guys to do all the work."

"Ah don't worry about it Alex. You earned it. What you did in there was amazing. He's going to be fine because of you. Besides, let's just say, you provided the entertainment." he said with an evil grin. "Something about black haired, blue eyed bad boys and lots of singing too!"

Alex closed her eyes in mortification, her face flamed red. She could picture her embarrassed face on public service posters for the evils of teenage drinking. Her head started to clear as the aspirin took hold. She opened her eyes and looked at her laughing friend.

"Ok, I deserve a little teasing for last night but that's enough." she thought to herself.

"Hey Josh, remember this? 'I would kill someone to keep you safe Dara.'" she said as a sickly sweet love declaration.

His face went from laughing to blank instantly. "Right, I'm done. Let's go check on Quinn, Doctor." he quickly changed the subject. She laughed at him and grabbed his hand as they went in to the clinic to check on Quinn.

Later that morning, once everyone was awake and they were eating a breakfast of instant oatmeal, they had a group meeting. Quinn had woken up with clear eyes and hungry for breakfast so the boys had carried him on his stretcher out onto the porch and propped his upper body up with pillows so he could eat with them. Alex didn't want his leg to be moved for a few days and they discussed what the plans would be.

Josh led the discussion. "I think we need to plan on staying here for at least five days. If we go back on the road with Quinn and we get attacked again, we would be in trouble. I looked through the house yesterday and it's untouched. I don't think anyone has been here. There are a lot of supplies we can use and take with us and there are some generators that I might be able to get working. I say we stay put until Quinn is more mobile and then we go like mad for the border and home. We've been staying away from main roads to avoid people and we've been shot at twice so it doesn't seem to be helping us. All this back road driving is just making us lose time. Once we leave here, I say we head towards the interstate and once we get past Great Falls we get on it and try and make better time. I know Alex, Quinn and I have all been to Great Falls with our families for shopping. I've never seen that part of the interstate, from the border to Great Falls with heavy traffic. What about you Quinn?"

Quinn didn't answer him because he had fallen asleep again. His head was slumped down, with his chin resting on his chest. They took the empty bowl off of his lap and eased his upper body back down onto the stretcher. They decided to leave him out on the porch in the fresh air so they covered him up with blankets and moved out into the yard to finish the discussion.

"I agree with you Josh. We need to stay here and let him heal. We were so lucky with where he was shot. Those bullets could have hit bone or even worse, his main artery. As it is he'll be limping for a long time. I'm done with this back road driving too. It's just taking too long and is just as dangerous. I agree that the northern part of the interstate was never very busy. There were always a lot of transport trucks and it was busy on a long weekend at the border crossing with shoppers but this happened on a Tuesday morning so it shouldn't be heavy with car crashes. I'm ready to get home so that's my vote." Alex told them. Cooper and Dara nodded their agreement.

"Alright then, we should go up to the house and get it ready. We might as well stay up there for the next few days in comfort. Once we get Quinn moved up into one of the bedrooms, I'll start working on the generators and see if we can get some power. We'll need more water too if we are here very long."

Dara volunteered to stay with Quinn as the rest went up to the house to get it ready for the coming days.

Chapter 18

Alex put her fork down and groaned at her stuffed belly. They had been on the Vet's property for three days since the operation and so far Quinn was doing much better. He was starting to complain about being bored and that his leg was itchy so Alex knew he was healing. She had switched him to Tylenol for the pain and packed up the stronger drugs for future emergencies. Josh had fashioned him a type of crutch and she was going to start him walking the next day. It had taken all the first day for Josh to get one of the generators working but with much cursing he had it done by dark. Unfortunately there was a fancy, hot water on demand system in the house and he couldn't do anything to make it work, so they had running water but still had to boil it.

On the second day Cooper and Josh had poked around in the barn and found an ATV that they got started. They had gone out into the fields to see if there were any neighbours close by that the group would have to deal with. They found that the property was surrounded by forest and they couldn't see any other homes. What they did come back with was very welcomed. At the back fence line there was a small stream that ran through the property and keeping close to it were six beef cows. When the water stopped feeding into their troughs they must have went to the stream to drink. Having been born and raised on a working farm, Josh had no problem rounding one up and getting it back to the barn.

When Josh showed the girls the cow and happily exclaimed,

"Dinner!"

Alex had clapped her hands in applause but Cooper and Dara just stared at him in confusion. When Josh saw that they didn't get it, he laughed and howled at them. "Where did you think steaks came from? They aren't born in little white foam trays covered in plastic wrap!" He laughed even harder at their shocked faces. When he got his breath back he reassured them "Don't worry about it. I'll take care of it, just have the barbeque warmed up in a few hours and we'll have a feast."

Cooper and Dara were excited for fresh red meat but were more than happy to leave the preparations in Josh's hands. All of their bodies were craving fresh protein and greens. They had been eating from cans for the past two weeks and the girls were thrilled to find potatoes that were still good in the basement pantry. The vegetables would be canned but it was still exciting to have fresh meat and potatoes. With the power on they could do their baking in the kitchens big oven and they moved from baking buns to baking loaves of bread. They still had plenty of flour in the camper but were pleased to find another big bag in the house.

Whoever had lived in the house had lived there alone. They had found only one bedroom that was being used with clothes in the closet. There were pictures of family members but only one man had lived in the house. Being out of town and in an isolated area seemed a strange place to have a business but the group was just happy to have a safe refuge while Quinn healed.

Josh stuffed the camper's small freezer with meat and then braved the stench of the house's refrigerators compartment. Alex helped him clean out all the spoiled rotten food and cleaned the insides with disinfectant before putting the fresh meat in it.

After an amazing feast of barbequed steak and baked potatoes, the girls brought out the cake they had baked in the house's oven and they all went into the living room to eat dessert. Alex had wrapped and splinted Quinn's leg so it wouldn't move and with help he could move from the dining table to an arm chair with an ottoman to prop up his leg.

Even with the generator working they couldn't use the huge flat screen TV that dominated one wall. It had fried with everything else that had a computer chip in it. It was still nice to just sit comfortably in a lighted room instead of around a campfire on the ground.

Quinn fell into a doze as soon as he was done eating his cake and Josh and Dara started a card game together. Cooper was flipping through a magazine so Alex decided to go outside and take a walk. She missed the routine of gymnastics and her body wanted exercise. She slipped out of the house and walked down the driveway, enjoying the cool evening air. Emily was on her mind and she tried to picture where her friend might be. Had she made it home yet? How long did it take to sail up the coast and cross one province to get home? She couldn't help but think of her family and what might be happening with them. As she came back up to the house she stopped at the edge of the wide lawn and decided she had to get her mind off home.

Alex slipped her boots and socks off and dropped down into some warm up stretches. When she felt her muscles were ready she launched herself across the lawn and sprang into hand springs and cartwheels. She kept it easy because of the grass and worked her way back and forth in different combinations. Everything faded away as she pushed her body through different tumbles and she had a light coating of sweat when she finally came to a stop. She did a few more stretches and went to pick up her boots. As she came to the stairs of the house she was jolted by Cooper who was standing by the railing.

Happy that the darkness would cover her blush, she wondered if he had been watching the whole time. She went up the stairs and sat on a deck chair to put her socks and boots back on.

"I used to watch you." he said quietly.

Her head snapped up from tying her boot and she stared at him in confusion.

"At school I mean. When you would practice your routines in the gym, I'd watch you. It's so amazing and beautiful the way you move from one flip to the next. It was like being able to see music. Ok, that sounded really dumb. Never mind." he mumbled and turned away, embarrassed.

"No, not dumb." Alex said standing and joining him at the rail "I think that's the nicest thing anyone's ever said to me. Thank you. I never saw you there."

"Yeah well, I didn't think you would be too happy about the local hoodlum spying on you so I stayed back out of sight."

Alex studied him for a minute and asked "So what's that all about anyways, the whole bad boy reputation?"

Cooper didn't respond for a while and Alex didn't think he was going to answer her until he finally said quietly, "It's a joke, a scam." Alex stayed quiet and waited. He turned to her and asked "Do you really want to know?"

When she nodded, he turned away and looked out over the lawn. "My Dad's an ass, a lowlife loser. He drinks too much, likes to be a bully and can't keep a real job. My Mom finally got fed up and left five years ago. I never had a lot of friends when I was younger and it got worse after my Mom left. So I've been a loner for a while. I mean, who wants to bring friends over to a dirty, dumpy house with a bully Dad around. So no one really knows much about me. Then a few years ago, I get a call from the bar to come get my Dad because he's drunk and stupid. I go over to the bar and the cops are loading him up into the back to take him home. They're feeling bad for me and offer a ride. So I'm climbing into the back of the cop car and some kids from school see me. That started the first rumours. Then I get suspended for fighting and that added to it. The truth was, I tried to stop this jerk jock from tormenting a freshman and he took a swing at me, so I put him down. After that the rumours were flying and I just kept my mouth shut and went with it.

Do you know I've had kids ask me if I could sell them drugs, or get them an IPod for cheap? It's such a joke. I've never broken the law in my life. My Dad has some creepy friends and the cops come by now and then asking questions. They all know me and know I'm not like my Dad, so when they see me walking they always stop and ask how I'm doing or if I want a ride somewhere.

Every time some kid sees that, it just fuels the rumours more. So it's all a scam. I've just been waiting for graduation to get out of here. I get really good grades and I think I can get a scholarship next year. At least I did, until all this happened."

Alex stood beside Cooper and they looked out at the lawn together, both lost in thought. After a while, Alex sighed in frustration "I don't get it. I'm a teenager and I don't understand teenagers, me included. Things can be so hard and confusing and we make it even worse for each other. Why are we so quick to sell each other out? Did you know Dara used to be one of my best friends growing up? She started to change when we hit junior high and I just let her go. All I saw was her crazy make-up and funky hair. I never tried to find out what was underneath it all, and now that we're back together, I can't imagine how we could ever not be friends. I never talked to you. I heard what was said about you and took it for fact and never gave you a chance. Why, why do we do that? We're all struggling with things and we're all scared sometimes so why do we make it even harder on each other?" she turned to Cooper and took his hand. "I'm sorry I never talked to you and I'm sorry I didn't make the effort to see who you are under the reputation. I'm so glad you came with us. I'm so glad I can say you are my friend." And she leaned in and kissed him softly on his cheek.

Cooper was humbled by this girl's kindness. He had watched her over the years and admired her but now he felt something even more for her. The question was, could he have a chance with her?"

Before he could say anything more, Josh came out onto the porch. He took in their closeness and raised an eyebrow. "Cooper, you want to help me get Quinn up to bed?"

"Sure man, of course." and he let go of Alex's hand and followed him in.

Alex stayed on the porch thinking for a while about Cooper and how easy it was to misjudge people.

** ** ** ** ** ** ** ** **

They had been at the Vet's clinic for six days and everyone was getting anxious to leave. They were all thinking about home and how close they were. When Quinn snapped at Alex for the third time over changing his bandages she had had enough. She called everyone out to the porch and helped Quinn down the stairs to the lawn. He was doing well getting around but stairs were still a problem. Once they were all gathered around she began.

"Ok we're all getting pissy about not being on the road so this is what I think. Tomorrow will have been a week since Quinn was shot and he's healing really fast, faster than I thought he would. So Quinn, if you can walk from here to the clinic without falling down or stopping, we leave in the morning. If you can't do it, we stay for a few more days. There's no point in leaving too soon only to have you re-injure your leg. A few more days of healing might make all the difference in a fight on the road, so give it your best shot. But seriously Quinn, if it's too much, stop. Don't push yourself too hard or we'll be here even longer."

Quinn looked around at all his friends who were giving him encouraging smiles and nodded. He kept his crutch with him as he walked towards the clinic but tried not to use it. He was almost there when he knew he wouldn't make it. He took another step but had to stop and lean on his crutch. He hung his head in misery as he heard his friends walk up behind him.

Alex came around in front of him and she had the biggest grin on her face, which confused him. She slipped under his arm to give him support and squeezed him tight.

"Holy crap! That was amazing! I can't believe how far you got. Great job Quinn!" she beamed happily.

"What are you talking about? You said I had to make it the whole way." he said to her in confusion as she helped lower him into a deck chair in front of the clinic.

"Well yeah, but I didn't even really think you'd make it half way. You've been such a jerk today, I mean, we all have, that I was trying to make a point.

Dude, you were shot, twice! It hasn't even been a week. We need to stop being so cranky and deal with it. But after seeing how far you came, well in my professional Doctor's opinion, I say…we leave in two days!"

Everyone cheered and Quinn started to laugh. He looked at Alex and said while laughing, "You are so mean."

The next two days were filled with busy activities. They stripped the house of all useful supplies and more importantly the clinic of its precious medical supplies. They pulled everything out of all the vehicles and repacked it all, leaving out some extra things they didn't feel were priorities. Josh and Cooper were determined to fit the ATV they had got working in the back of the van. They had all been practicing everyday with the assault rifles after finding out there were no other properties around that would hear them and they were all getting better at controlling the weapon. The semiautomatic setting was the best option as it let off three round bursts and didn't speed through the ammunition clips so fast.

They boiled pot after pot of water and took baths and washed their clothes. Quinn kept exercising and stretching his leg in small bursts to avoid overtiring it. Alex and Dara baked cookies and buns and filled Tupperware with the baked goods. They still had two more cases of yeast packages and plenty of powdered eggs and milk. They didn't know what would happen at the border but they wanted to be prepared for bribes or a fight. It was amazing what a bag of buns would do to a person's attitude after weeks of a steady diet of canned food.

After topping up their water tanks and bottles, they were ready to go and Alex couldn't sleep. They were leaving in the morning and they had had another huge meal with cherry pie for dessert, made from a can of pie filling she had found when cleaning out the pantries. She was anxious to get over the border. There really wasn't all that much different about the two countries but something about being in her own country soothed her. After tossing and turning for an hour, she gave up and went downstairs. She wandered around the main floor for a while and finally went out onto the front porch.

Quinn was sitting in a chair with his rifle propped up beside him. "Hey Alex, what are you doing up?" he asked when she sat in the chair beside him.

"Can't sleep, too keyed up about leaving, I guess. What about you, isn't Josh supposed to be on watch tonight?"

"Yeah, but I convinced him to let me do it. I've had so much sleep the past week that I'd just lay there staring at the ceiling." He reached over and took her hand. "I'm glad you're up. There's been something I wanted to say to you. What you did for me, taking the bullets out of my leg was amazing. I just wanted to say thank you. You mean so much to me. I don't know if I could have made it this far without you." he said staring at her intensely.

"Hey, of course you would. Someone would have manned up and carved your leg up for you." she joked.

"No, that's not what I mean, getting this far from California, and making our way home. You kept me going. I love Josh like a brother and Dara and Cooper are good friends but all I've focused on is keeping you safe and getting you home. When those bikers had us, what they said they were going to do to you, it almost drove me mad. The thought of you being hurt like that killed me." When Alex didn't say anything, he asked her "You must know how I feel about you after all these years, Alex."

Alex's mind was a spiralling mess of confusion and panic. First Cooper and now Quinn, she had to stay off this porch, it was a dangerous place to be. She closed her eyes and breathed deep. She could feel Quinn looking at her, waiting for a response. She opened her eyes and looked into his.

"When I saw you covered in blood in the back of that truck, my heart stopped and I saw flashbacks of us together over the years. I love you Quinn. I have loved you for years and if I lost you, a piece of me would die. But I don't know if I'm ready to make us more. Everything is so crazy and messed up. All the things we've gone through and we still aren't even home. I'm just not ready for more right now."

"Is it Cooper? Do you like him? I've seen the way he looks at you and I understand because I look at you the same way." he said.

"I...I don't know!" she laughed in frustration. "The world as we know it is over and I'm supposed to pick which boy to go to prom with?! I can't Quinn! Yes, Cooper has feelings for me and I might have some for him but I Do Not Know! This isn't something I can do right now. Please be my friend and love me like I love you but just leave it for now. We can work it out when we get home, okay?" she pleaded.

He sat back and smiled reassuringly at her. He gave her hand a squeeze and said "It's ok Alex, I just wanted to tell you how I felt and you're right. This isn't the time for it and I love you too. You should try and get some sleep. We're out of here first thing in the morning."

She stood up and leaned down to kiss him on the cheek but he turned his head and their lips met softly. Her whole body lit up and she pulled back in surprise with her eyes wide. He gave her a smug little grin "I just thought you should know. Good night Alex."

She stumbled back towards the front door and mumbled a "Good night" to him. All she could think was "Now I'm never going to fall asleep."

Chapter 19

They left at dawn, excited to finally be on the road again. They made their way back and forth across the Montana countryside avoiding the few towns they came close to but always headed north. It was late in the afternoon when they finally circled around Great Falls and headed towards the interstate. Just as they thought, the interstate was wide open with mainly transport trucks left abandoned on the road. Almost all had their trailer doors open and goods were strewn all over the ground around them.

They had discussed when the best time to approach the border would be and they decided that morning would be best. They knew there were many small back roads that they could use to cross over the border but they were all familiar with the Coutts/Sweetgrass crossing. They also hoped that they would be able to get information on the state of their country if the border crossing was still being controlled by guards.

They stopped about an hour's drive from the border and set up camp well off the road. They hadn't seen any other working cars on the way or any people walking but they were still cautious. Alex tried to stay with Dara while they set up and made supper. She didn't want to be caught alone by Quinn or Cooper. She wasn't ready to talk to either one of them until she figured out things in her head.

Dara turned and almost bumped into Alex for the second time and finally clued in. With a laugh she asked her "What are you doing Alex? If you get any closer to me we can both wear these pants."

"Sorry, sorry." She did a quick look around and saw the boys were busy with something in the back of the van so she told Dara "I'm avoiding Quinn and Cooper. If I'm not alone, they won't go all gaga on me so I'm being your shadow."

Dara threw her head back and laughed causing Josh to look her way with a smile. "Oh, that's good. We're in the middle of the apocalypse and you're stuck in some bad CW network love triangle? Oh that's hilarious!" and she laughed even more.

Alex mock glared at her friend. It was kind of funny though and she finally couldn't hold a straight face anymore and started laughing too. When they finally got control of themselves, Dara wiped her eyes and looked at her friend "Seriously? Both of them?"

Alex nodded with a roll of her eyes. "Ridiculous, right? I'm mean, I haven't had a date in months and NOW I have two guys chasing me?"

Dara shook her head, "Wow, I thought I had it bad but you win hands down."

"What? What's going on with you...Oh, Josh, right?"

"Yeah, I know he likes me but do you think the guy will say anything or even better, make a move? No, not one thing and it's driving me crazy! I will never understand men."

"Well, with Josh I think you're going to have to make the first move. For all his joking and pranks, I know he's shy with girls. I don't think he's even been on a date before. Sorry Dara, this one's going to be all on you."

"I kind of figured that out. So what are you going to do? Cooper or Quinn, what a choice!"

"Don't remind me! I don't plan on doing anything but avoiding the whole sticky mess until we get home. I like them both but it's not something I can figure out as we're traveling like this and that's what I told Quinn last night. The only good thing about it is there doesn't seem to be any hard feelings between the two of them and I really want to keep it that way, especially while we're on the road. So, you are now my shadow buddy and I plan to stick to you like glue!" She gave Dara a sickly sweet smile and batted her eyes at her.

Dara groaned "That's great! Now I'll never get anywhere with Josh!" she laughed.

"Hey, you help me out here and I'll set up some alone time for you two. Isn't it great to be friends again and help each other out with these little girlfriend issues?" Alex said mockingly.

"You know what Alex? It really is. I missed you a lot." she said, no longer joking.

Alex pulled her into a hug and whispered "Me too."

They decided not to have a camp fire that night and everyone took a turn at keeping watch. They were so close to being home they didn't want anything to go wrong. They were up early the next morning and quickly packed up after a hasty breakfast.

The closer they got to the border the more car wrecks they saw. They could see the cluster of buildings ahead and they could also make out groups of people and what looked like tents and campers clustered around the parking lots. It looked like most of the cars had been moved out of the road ahead but there was a line of them being used to block the actual crossing lanes. Josh pulled the truck to a stop before they got to the main group of people. They quickly got out and gathered by Quinn who was in the truck's front passenger seat. People were already looking their way but no one was approaching them yet. Quinn stayed in the truck but had his window down.

"Ok, it looks like they aren't letting these people through for some reason. We are crossing this border no matter what so get your passports ready. Everyone sling a rifle and make sure you have extra clips. We don't want to start a fight here but we will finish one if we have too. This is what we do. We drive straight up and stop in front of one of the crossing booths. Everyone will get out except Cooper, who will be up on the camper covering us. We show them our passports and maybe offer a bag of buns to sweeten them up. Keep your rifles on their slings unless we are threatened. These guys will all be armed as well and we don't want to seem too threatening. Make sure you lock the doors when you get out. We don't want one of these people trying to steal our rides. Stay close and keep going until we get up there. If anyone tries to get in the

way just blow the horn and keep going. Everybody agree?"
They all nodded and ran back to their vehicles.

Once Josh saw everyone was ready he pulled ahead.
They weren't going very fast but kept a steady pace. Josh
had to blow his horn once when three men tried to get in
front of them and wave them down but they scattered
when they saw he wasn't stopping and if that wasn't
enough, the hard look and barrel of the assault rifle he
stuck out the window and pointed their way was. The
people lining the road all stopped what they were doing
and watched the kids go by. There were little camp sites
set up all along the road and from the amount of trash
everywhere, they had been here for a while. More and
more people were emerging from tents and campers to see
what the new arrivals would do.

Alex noted that a lot of older people were in the
crowd, especially around the campers, and she guessed
that they were Canadian snow birds who spent the winters
down south. They must be trying to get back home. They
came to a stop in front of a disabled car that was blocking
the guard booth and they all climbed out and locked the
vehicles. Except for Cooper, who stayed in the camper and
scanned the crowd from the roof. There were only six
guards on the other side of the barricade and as they came
closer Alex could see that they were wearing Canadian
uniforms.

Alex was so happy to see people in authority who
were actually doing their jobs that she gave them a big
smile and waved. Her smile went away when the obvious
leader started to shake his head with a scowl on his face.
He marched up to the other side and stopped.

He looked them all over and pronounced, "Border's
closed! Turn those vehicles around and move them away
from here."

Josh pretended he hadn't heard him "We have our
passports right here sir! We're all Canadians and we have
nothing to declare." he tried joking while holding his
passport out.

The man didn't even reach for it and without a change of expression told them "It doesn't matter. The border is closed. NO one gets across."

Josh scanned the faces of the five other guards and saw they were all looking sympathetic and some even frustrated. Before he could say anything else, Alex stepped forward and turned on the charm.

"Sir, we understand you're just doing your job. We're just so happy to see the Canadian authorities after everything we've been through. Would you and your men like some fresh baked buns? We made them in our camper's oven." She smiled sweetly and held out a grocery bag filled with buns. The man leaned forward and his eyes were greedy as he took in how many buns were in the bag. As he went to reach for the handles he came face to face with Alex's assault rifle barrel, right between his eyes.

Alex had also seen the sympathetic looks the other guards had given them and hoped they wouldn't do anything rash. She gave them a cutesy smile and focused back on the leader with a hard look and said in an impressive voice "Now you listen to me! We are Canadian citizens that just want to go home! We were in Disneyland when this happened and we went through hell to get here but we fought our way through it. You are not going to stop me from going home and you should be ashamed of yourself for trying. If all these people out here are Canadians and you stopped them from going home then you Sir, are a traitor to your country and the people you are supposed to serve. Now, tell me again why we can't cross this border."

The other guards hadn't moved and a few were even smirking at their leader's predicament. The man looking down Alex's rifle barrel was red in the face and his eyes were very angry.

"It's standard procedure to shut the border down in a nationwide emergency. We are following what the manual says. Now put that down, little girl. You're not even big enough to fire it." the man snarled as he reached for his side arm.

Josh said "Uh oh. Shouldn't have said that." to the man in warning, as all the teens brought their guns up and pointed them at him.

Alex was done, just plain done with condescending idiots like this. She pressed her gun barrel hard between his eyes and roared at him.

"Mister I might have been a little girl when we left Disneyland but when me and my friends killed a group of bikers in Nevada, I stopped being one. Now take your hand away from that weapon or I'll give you a third eye."

The man paled at her words and put his hands up.

"You did the right thing closing the border when it happened, but that was over twenty days ago. So, as a Canadian citizen and taxpayer who helps pay your wages, I'm here to tell you that you are FIRED!" she glanced towards the other guards, "Any of you have a problem with that?" When the other officers shook their heads, she continued, "Good, do any of you have restraints?"

One of the guards stepped forward, "Yes Ma'am, I got some right here."

"Thank you sir. Please restrain this man before he gets himself shot. You can let him go after these people have all been cleared through." she told him.

As the guard came over and took his boss's gun off him Alex was surprised at how quiet it was. She turned and looked at the crowd of people behind her. They were all watching and waiting in silence.

One of the other border guards walked over to Alex and her friends "Excuse me Miss but did you say you took out a group of bikers in Nevada?" When they all nodded their heads, the man's face split in a huge grin "Holy crap! Are you guys the Maple Leaf Mafia?"

They all stared at the man in shock. Josh started to howl with laughter "I told you it was a catchy name!" In the silence of the waiting crowd, everyone heard what was said and at Josh's reply the crowd let out a huge cheer.

After discussing things with the group of border guards they helped to get things moving. They had the guards open two channels through the crossing. One was for Canadians with any form of ID that had an address in Canada and one for people who claimed to be Canadians but had no identification.

The new leader walked with Josh and told him "I've wanted to do that for a while. We shut everything down on the first day as per procedure but as the days went by and people started showing up with passports we all felt it was wrong not to let them through. We have a hardened radio that still worked and we spoke to the military but they were pretty busy and didn't offer much help."

Josh looked sharply at the man "The Canadian military is still functioning? What's going on in our country?"

"Well I don't know much but what we've heard on the radio isn't pretty. The pulse stopped up north, just past Edmonton and straight across the country but we don't have a whole lot of population up there. The major cities in the East are gutted. You couldn't pay me to get near Toronto or anywhere in Quebec. Calgary and Edmonton are bad but a lot of people just walked out so the countryside around any city is also a mess. We have heard a lot of small towns with radios saying things about barricading against refugees and other places have set up aid stations - but with no food being shipped in and the growing season just starting, there will be a lot of deaths in the next few months. The prairie provinces are lucky because they don't have huge populations and there's a lot of livestock, but if it's not managed right it won't matter. So where are you guys headed? Where's home?" he asked

"Our town's called Prairie Springs. It's in Central Alberta, about an hour west of Red Deer."

The guard made a face "Prairie Springs, Prairie Springs, I heard something about that town a few days ago. There was some chatter on the radio about it." He paused to try and remember and shook his head. "I don't know. It was some warning about staying away from it. We were changing the dial and I just caught a moment of it, sorry." They came to the line of people who wanted to cross with no identification and the guard sighed "Now how am I going to work this mess out? Things are going to be hard enough up north without a flood of hungry Americans coming in, but how do we figure that out?"

Josh studied the people waiting in line and saw the first was a family of four with a small boy and girl. He grinned at the guard and said, "Follow my lead."

He stepped up to the family and crouched down in front of the kids "Hey there guys, you ready to go home?" They both nodded shyly. "Are these your parents? Do you live in Canada?" When the kids both nodded he smiled at them "Ok you have to pass a test. Are you ready? Here it is. What do you call a dollar in Canada?"

The little boy grinned a gapped tooth smile and yelled "A loonie!"

Josh nodded and stood.

"Pass!"

He moved down to the next and greeted the woman "Ma'am, can you tell us a Canadian football team?"

She looked at him in confusion and answered, "Sure, there's the Stampeders, the BC Lions, the…"

Josh cut her off with, "Pass!"

The next people in line were a couple and he asked the woman "What party did you vote for in the last election?"

She answered without even thinking "Democrat."

Josh shook his head and made a sound like a buzzer, "EEEEE not in Canada, fail! Back of the line for you!" he left them sputtering and moved on to the next group.

There were six senior citizens grouped together. He smiled and nodded at them and asked, "What drive thru do you all get your coffee from?"

They all started to laugh and said in unison, "Tim Horton's!" with a few "Double Double's" thrown in as well.

Josh laughed with them and turned to the guard "Pass! Do you get the picture here?"

The guard shook his head in laughter. "Now that is streamlining the bureaucratic process my friend!"

After that, the group of teens loaded up and went through the check point. As they crossed in to Canada they all let out a cheer and some even had tears rolling down their faces.

Chapter 20

The three vehicles easily detoured around Lethbridge and Fort Macleod which were the two closest cities to the border. They got on Highway Two and headed north. This highway ran straight up through the province and passed through Calgary, Red Deer and Edmonton. It was the equivalent of the American Interstate but with less car wrecks due to the lower population. Other than detouring around Calgary, a city with a population well over a million, they were done with back road driving. They wanted to go home. Before the lights went out, it would have been a six hour drive but they kept their speed down and kept alert for ambushes. None of the kids were very concerned about trouble as Canada had very strict gun laws and unlike the American population, the average citizen didn't have hand guns or assault rifles. There were still plenty of hunting rifles and shot guns in the area, but nothing like in America.

As they traveled down the highway through field after field they were happy to see people out working in them. There were a few farm machines working in fields that looked like they had been taken from museums. A few people stopped working when they heard the cars go by and waved. None of the kids could stop smiling at the sight of crops being planted. This area would have food before too long.

They circled around Calgary and weren't surprised to see trash and dropped belongings everywhere. As people walked away from the city and headed out to the countryside looking for food, they had abandoned suitcases and other belongings that had become too much of a burden to carry.

There were bodies lying on the side of the road where people had just given up and sat down to die. Other bodies showed signs of a more violent end. After getting around

Calgary without a problem they stopped and made the decision to cut across diagonally towards their town. The corridor between Calgary, Red Deer and Edmonton was always heavy with traffic and they decided to take secondary highways the rest of the way. It was an easy trip and they were approaching a small town about an hour's drive from their home when they decided to stop and see if they could find out any news about their town. Josh had told the others about what the guard had heard on the radio and they all wanted more information instead of just going in blind.

There was the now routine road block on the outskirts of the town that was being manned by three guards. They pulled to a stop and they all climbed out and approached the barricade. The three men didn't seem all that concerned by the group and none of them aimed their weapons at the kids. The teens had all left their assault rifles in their vehicles but all still had side arms in holsters.

Quinn limped ahead and waved at the men. "Hello! We're headed up to Prairie Springs and we were hoping for some news of the town's status. Will we be able to travel through or do we have to back track around your town?" he asked in a respectful voice.

The oldest man studied Quinn thoughtfully and asked, "Aren't you Harry Dennison's grandson, Quinn?"

Quinn grinned and thought, "It's good to be home where everyone knows everyone."

"Yes Sir, I am. My friends and I got caught in the States on a school trip when the lights went out and we're just trying to make our way home. Do you have news about my family?"

"Well, that sounds like a heck of a tale to hear, if you kids came all the way up from the States. I haven't heard anything about your Granddad but we've heard some things about the town. Hold your hats for a minute and we'll move this car out of the way. You can give me a lift into the town center where we set up a meeting place and we'll tell you all we know."

The man waved the other two guards over and they quickly pushed the broken down car out of the road. When Dara pulled the truck through the road block the older man climbed into the back and they headed into town.

As they drove past homes, they could see many people busy at work. Most of the front lawns of homes had been ripped up and planted as gardens. There were groups of people standing in line with jugs and buckets waiting for water at a pump station. There was another area with tables set up and huge pots of steaming water where people were washing clothes. As they pulled up to the town's meeting area they could all smell meat cooking on a barbeque. There were four giant grills set up in a row and each was manned by cooks.

They got out and locked their doors out of habit. The older man led them towards the dining area and took a deep smell of the cooking meat. "Good timing on your part, supper will be ready in about twenty minutes. You kids must be starved for some red meat." he smiled proudly at the barbeques.

"Actually sir, we would be happy to contribute our own meat so as not to put a strain on the towns food supply" Quinn offered.

The man gave him a sharp look "Now you kids didn't steal some poor farmers stock did you? We won't abide looters in this town."

Quinn laughed "No, no, we butchered a cow in Montana. The property was abandoned and the cows were going feral. We have a fridge freezer in the camper and brought some with us." he assured the man.

The man nodded his head "Alright then, good thinking!" he held out his hand to shake, "Name's Tom Jacobson. I've got a place just outside of town but we finished planting it yesterday so I came in to town today for some company. We have a communal supper every day for everyone who works in the fields." He looked around his town with pride. "Yup we've done real well here. Lots of refugees walked in from the city but we made it clear there would be no free ride. We all work to get the crops planted and we'll all eat. I imagine we'll have to tighten our belts between now and harvest but we'll get by."

"Oh there's Mike now! He's been organizing everything around here and will know the latest on Prairie Springs. Mike! Hey Mike, I got some people you need to meet over here." he yelled.

Mike made his way over to the group and introductions were made all around. He grimaced when he heard where the kids were headed.

"We don't know a lot but what we've heard isn't good. About five days into the emergency, a group of gang bangers and hard cases went into town and took it over. They had fifty or so men and they were all armed. They went out to the farms and rounded everyone up and put them in one place. That's all we really know. Everyone that walks that way comes back with stories of being shot at from roadblocks and anyone with a working vehicle that goes there doesn't come back at all."

"I'm sorry kids. I wish I could tell you more but we just don't know what's happening there. The only other thing I've heard is that they are out planting the fields but no one can get close enough to get more news." He gave them a sad smile "You guys are welcome to stay here if you want."

The group was silent, trying to absorb what they had just heard. Quinn nodded to Mike "Thank you sir. We would be grateful if we could stay the night in your town but I think we will head that way tomorrow and scout things out." He looked around at his friends and they all nodded.

"Fair enough, welcome to Abbotsville. Please enjoy supper with us." he smiled and headed back to work.

There wasn't much to say after that and the kids wandered back to their camper to get cleaned up and grab supplies to contribute to the communal supper.

** ** ** ** ** ** ** ** **

The next morning the group was hidden in a forested area a few miles outside of their town. They were studying the manned road block through binoculars. They each took a good look at the men and surrounding area and passed them on to the next. When Cooper looked closely at the men he grunted.

"I know one of those guys! He's a friend of my Dad's. Not a big shock that he's working with the bad guys. His name's Buddy and he's a real loser. He's been in jail for lots of petty crime, everything from break and entering to drugs."

When everyone had taken a good look they moved back deeper into the forest. They were lucky that two sides of the town faced forest that went all the way to the mountains. There were a lot of campgrounds and a few lakes throughout the area. They were all familiar with the forest around their town and had spent many years having adventures in it. Their vehicles were parked well back at a little used camping area that didn't offer any camping services except a water hand pump. The hike to the town had taken under an hour as they had brought the bikes with them and only had to walk part of the way.

Once they were well back into the forest they discussed their next move. Cooper was thinking hard on a decision and finally put it to the group.

"I think I should go talk to Buddy. He knows me and he'll probably tell me what's going on. The only problem is that they might think I would want to join them. If my old man has joined with them it could be our way into town. The problem is I can't be a part of what they're doing so I would end up giving myself away. What do you guys think?"

Alex's first thought was, "NO WAY." She didn't want Cooper going in there and getting himself killed when the gang figured out he wasn't on their side, but before she could say anything Quinn spoke up.

"Do you think you can get information out of him and he'll let you leave? If you played it like you didn't care about the town but you didn't want to get involved in the gang? Would he let you turn around and go?"

Cooper thought about it hard. They needed information and he felt like he owed it to his new friends to help anyway he could.

"I think he would. He was always trying to be my pal and telling me not to follow in his and my Dad's footsteps. I really think I could get the info and then leave. I'm willing to take the chance."

Alex stepped forward and pulled him into a tight hug. She closed her eyes and said into his ear "Thank you. Please come back." She quickly released him and turned away.

He nodded to the others and handed Josh his automatic rifle. He kept his hand gun in its holster and shouldered a back pack. They all walked back to where they had left the bikes and he climbed onto his.

"If I get pulled into the town, watch for me on the west side by the forest and I'll try to make contact." With that he pedalled away.

Alex couldn't bear to watch him leave so she headed back into the woods to where they could see the road block.

Cooper was beyond nervous. The last thing he wanted was to get sucked into his Dad's lifestyle but he felt he had to do this for his friends. He had been alone for so long with no friends. The past twenty three days had been so amazing for him. The way they all worked together and watched each other's backs had filled a part of him he hadn't known was empty. And Alex, well if he ever had a chance to be with her, he would have to prove to her and himself that he was worth someone so good.

As he got closer to the roadblock he could see Buddy raise a hunting rifle up to his face. He should be able to see Cooper very well through its scope; at least he hoped he would. Cooper kept going, waiting for the sound of the shot that never came.

When he was close enough he yelled out "Hey Buddy, is that you? It's Cooper!"

Buddy motioned him to stop where he was and turned to talk to the other men. He came out from behind the cars and walked down the road to him. He had a surprised look on his face when he walked up.

"What the hell, Cooper! Aren't you supposed to be in California? What are you doing here?" he asked with an uncomfortable look on his face.

Cooper grinned sheepishly "Well yeah, but I ditched the kiddy trip at the airport and was hanging with some friends in the city when the lights went out. We've been partying it up but things got a little hot for me there, so I bounced and headed home. What's up with you? The cops got you working guard duty? No way man!" he said with a laugh.

Buddy didn't laugh but he looked over his shoulder back at the other men. He leaned close to Cooper and said quickly "All the cops are dead, man. A group of hard core guys came in and took over. They're using all the towns' people and farmers as slave labour. It's a real bad scene. Listen, I got bad news for you brother. Your Dad is dead. He thought he should be the big man around here cause he's the one who told these guys about the town's set up and the Boss man shot him like a dog. You need to jet! There's nothing here for you and you don't want them to find out who your old man was. Go find somewhere else."

"Ah shit! He never could keep his mouth shut." Cooper shook his head sadly. "But Buddy, how can a few guys hold all those people without them fighting back?"

Buddy checked over his shoulder again before answering him. "They got like sixty guys and they're holding a lot of the women and all the kids in the community center. It's real ugly Cooper. Now get out of here before they come check you out." He waved him back down the road.

"Yeah, I hear you. I'm out of here. Hey Buddy, one more thing. Did any of those kids make it back from California?"

Buddy smirked, "No way they'd make it back here. All those kids are dead by now. Count yourself lucky you ditched. Take care, Cooper. Sorry about your Dad."

Cooper nodded and turned his bike around. He headed back down the road towards his friends. He thought about his Dad being dead and thought he should feel something. He searched his heart and was saddened by finding only relief.

The group was waiting when he got back. They were all out of breath from running when they saw him heading back away from town.

Cooper told them everything he had learned and they all sat down to try and process the state of their home. Alex looked around at her friends. Dara was quietly crying and Josh was holding her hand and staring miserably at the ground. Quinn was looking off into the forest with an angry expression. Cooper was looking at Alex with a sympathetic frown. When she met his eyes he asked, "What do you want to do?"

Alex stood and looked at all her friends again. Then she picked up her rifle and spoke in a strong, clear voice.

"We fight!"

End of Book One

Coming Soon
Sea
A Stranded Novel

Emily and her friends headed to the California coast to find a boat back to Canada. They all felt that it would be much easier and quicker to sail home rather than go over land. They were wrong. Not only will they have to fight their way through the lawless city and the terrifying ocean, they will have a journey of hardship and loss as the biggest threat will come from within their own group. The trip home will change them all for good and bad as they are stranded at |SEA.

12901465R00105

Made in the USA
Charleston, SC
05 June 2012